MW01076108

WAITING
TO BE HEARD

WAITING TO BE HEARD

Youth Speak Out about Inheriting a Violent World

BY THE STUDENTS OF
THURGOOD MARSHALL ACADEMIC HIGH SCHOOL

PUBLISHED IN CONJUNCTION WITH
THE ISABEL ALLENDE FOUNDATION
AND 826 VALENCIA

Published May 2004 by 826 Valencia
in conjunction with the Isabel Allende Foundation

Copyright © 2004 by 826 Valencia

Volunteer editorial board: June Jackson, Kate Kudirka,
Brigid O'Neil, Pavla Popavich, and Karen Schaser.

Volunteer editors-at-large: Shannon Bryant, Mary Colgan,
Malaika Costello-Dougherty, Norman Patrick Doyle, Anastasia Goodstein,
Micaela Heekin, Abigail Jacobs, Andy Jones, Monica Maduro, Maggie Mason,
Tom Molanphy, Abner Morales, Amie Nenninger, Matt Ness, Jessica Partch,
Pavla Popovich, Mary Schaefer, Kellie Schmitt, Jennifer Traig, and Vicky Walker.

Book design and production: Alvaro Villanueva

Photography: Eve Eckman

Printed in Canada by Westcan Printing Group

ACKNOWLEDGMENTS

This book required thousands of hours of work from a small army of students, teachers, tutors and other volunteers. First of all, the students spent an absolutely stunning amount of time making sure their essays were the best they could be. They worked in class, at home, and many, many days after school, one-on-one with 826 Valencia tutors, shaping their ideas and editing their work. They were late to sports practices, they skipped innumerable social activities, they stayed up late and traveled across the city to 826 Valencia—all to make sure their words were perfect. And when we consider that the majority of the students in this book are seniors, who were not able to even include this book in their college-application materials, their devotion becomes all the more remarkable.

On behalf of 826 Valencia and the Isabel Allende Foundation, we'd like to thank Jesse Madway, the English and History instructor at Thurgood Marshall High School who spearheaded this project, and whose tireless commitment to this book, and to his students, is a marvel to behold. Robert Roth, a 11th grade history teacher, worked with Mr. Madway, giving the original writing prompt to all of his students and working with the students on their original compositions. He was heroic in his support for the endeavor. Chuck Raznikov, also a history teacher at Thurgood Marshall, assisted in many ways.

Over the course of about three months, 826 Valencia sent adult tutors into Thurgood Marshall, to meet regularly with students and help them with their ideas, with the shaping of their essays and finally with line editing. We all spent many afternoons at Thurgood Marshall, and the sight was inspiring—a whole classroom full of students working with the tutors, each pair hunched over a piece of paper, making it right. The tutors' work was invaluable. Their names: Jason Biehl, Andrea Countryman, Peter Crowell, Norman Doyle, Marcie Dresbaugh, Eve Ekman, Laura Fraenza, Anastasia Goodstein,

Yosh Han, June Jackson, Ellen Johnson, Evan Kennedy, Meaghan Kimball, William Laven, Chad Lent, Celine Lombardi, John McMurtrie, Sierra Melcher, Tom Molanphy, Abner Morales, Monica Norton, Edward Opton, Sue Pierce, Pavla Popovich, Nicki Richesin, Quressa Robinson, Kat Rochemont, Sage Romano, Mary Schaefe, Laura Scholes, Kellie Schmitt, Cliff Stanley, Marla Stever, Jeanne Stock, Christy Susman, Rob Tocalino, Susan Tu, Chloe Veltman, Andy Wong, Elizabeth Zambelli.

Thanks also go to the following tutors, who also attended the student editorial meetings at 826 Valencia, helping the students shape the collection as a whole: June Jackson, Brigid O'Neil, Pavla Popavich, and Karen Schaser. Quressa Robinson, 826 Valencia's in-schools coordinator, managed the daunting feat of organizing all of the tutors and teachers. Alvaro Villanueva handled all the production aspects of making this book, and became a friend and mentor to the students in the process. Julia White, Tracy Barrerio and Susan Tu, all on the staff of 826 Valencia, also were instrumental in making this book a reality.

Finally, we'd like to thank Isabel Allende and Lori Barra, the executive director of Isabel Allende Foundation. This project was their idea. They came to us at 826 Valencia, asking if we would coordinate a student book on the issue of peace, offering to fund it completely. Because we had worked with Jesse Madway and Thurgood Marshall High School before, and both because the high school knows firsthand about issues of peace and violence and because the students and teachers we've known there are so hardworking and inspiring, we knew they would be the perfect school.

We are endlessly proud to be part of this collection, which we find illuminating, unsettling, heartbreaking, and thoroughly inspiring.

Ninive Calegari, Director, 826 Valencia
Dave Eggers, Founder, 826 Valencia

STOP AND LISTEN

by Isabel Allende

Against a backdrop of war and terrorism, which seems to be the mark of our time, hearing what our kids have to say about violence breaks your heart. Their voices are loud and clear. Pay attention, for they have so much to say!

My generation grew up during the Cold War. We feared a nuclear cataclysm that would end life on this planet. Such an awesome disaster was impossible to imagine, it was an abstract threat, like hell. But there is nothing abstract about our kids' fears today. They are growing up surrounded by violence, they do not have to imagine it because they are exposed to it in their homes, schools, and streets. Our culture has a morbid fascination with aggression, weapons, war, and crime—the more gruesome the better. The most successful public speakers are mass murderers. Even our favorite sports are about guys almost killing each other for a ball. Privileged kids experience the thrill of violence vicariously—video games, movies, music, sports— but most children in the world, including most children in our own country and in our own neighborhood, experience it firsthand. They live in fear.

Students at Thurgood Marshall Academic High School, which serves San Francisco's tough Bayview/Hunters Point neighborhood, were given a chance to speak about peace. The school was in the press in October 2002 because, after a fight among students, fifty police officers went into the campus, batons in hand, to take care of the "riot." The kids called it an "invasion." The school was closed for a week afterward. In recent times there have been shootings in the neighborhood involving classmates and former students. Many at Thurgood Marshall are children of immigrants and refugees, they come from, or have roots, in places around the world that are ravaged by violence. No wonder that, when given the chance to speak their minds, they did not choose peace as their central theme, but the other side of the coin: violence. They can dream of peace, they may even be able to imagine how peace looks like, but they wrote about violence because that is what they know best. It all started with a question asked to the whole school by two committed teachers: "How can peace be achieved in such a violent world?" That got the students thinking, talking, and writing. The result of months and months of hard work, of innumerable drafts and much editing, are these pages. The young authors of this extraordinary book write about the ugly reality of violence in their lives. They are sad and angry, but not impotent. Sometimes they are on their knees, but each time they are able to get back on their feet. They are as afraid of walking in the streets of their city as they are concerned about the globe. They write about what they have witnessed, and they also write about how they see the world. One of them is afraid of not making it home one day because of a shooting on the bus. Another one asks: "How is it right for the U.S. government to punish the people who use violence as a solution, when it is exactly the same solution the government uses?" A student talks about the perfect idea of how the world should be that her little sister has. She wants to protect her sister. She adds: "I can't wait to grow up and live in this crazy world, just so that I can change it." A girl addresses her mom to ask about her father, who was murdered, and says that she lives her life carefully, not to step on any toes, constantly aware of the possibility of violence. A boy describes the sound of wood against bone, referring to the sticks the police used at the schoolyard. And another child writes with amazing lucidity: "On Sept. 11, I felt sad and powerless to stop what had occurred. I wanted retaliation and revenge as much as the next person. Yet, as the war on terrorism continued, I felt no sense of achievement or happiness. None of this helped me feel better about myself. All I saw before me was more bloodshed, terror, and deaths, and I felt horror at how we could have caused this much destruction."

To me the most fascinating aspect of this book is that it fully represents the kids' state of mind. They had total freedom to express themselves and as much command over the project as possible. A couple of formidable teachers and the many volunteers of 826 Valencia helped them, but they did the rest. The students came up with the title and the themes: voices of hope, conscience, love, misunderstanding, empowerment, survival, and many others. There was no previous idea of how the book should be, and therefore the result is very subjective. There are two pieces about the struggle of Palestinian people, for example, but none about Israelis was submitted. Most of these essays are based on the kids' relationship with conflict and violence, but all of these teenagers are capable of seeing the state of the world beyond their personal experience. They seem determined to change things, for they don't like what they will inherit.

I know that the opportunity to express their thoughts and be heard has empowered these young people. That is the beauty of the written word: it changes you and it may change others. That has been my case. Telling my own story has given me strength, as I am sure that was the case of the authors of these essays. These teenagers are smart, brave, and very inspiring. Their words move me deeply and also fill me with optimism. I trust that these and other kids will grow up with a vision of the future and the courage to make that vision possible. They will not be discouraged or beaten to submission.

One of the students at Thurgood Marshall summarized the book for me. She imagined an ideal newspaper where all the good news would be displayed on the front page and the bad news at the bottom in small print. This is a title on the first article, large print: THERE IS STILL HOPE OUT THERE!

INTRODUCTION

by

Jing Chen, Shirley Chen, Michael Jordan, Yasmin Khalil,
Rosanna Lin, Zikang Liu, Eric Yili Miao, & Wanda Sarah Seto

We are sophomores, juniors, and seniors at Thurgood Marshall Academic High School who were given a simple assignment from our teacher, asking us to "explore the ways that we think about conflict, violence, and peace in our world." Since then, we have gone through countless drafts and months of hard work to make this book the way it is. *Waiting to Be Heard* is a collection of our writings on this subject.

The title of this book reflects our feeling that the world is run by adults, and that we're supposed to take over some day, but until that day comes, nobody seems to be listening to what we have to say. But there is something to be said. There is an urgency to try to keep getting our voices out, and this book gives us a chance to voice our opinions. We are the future and we have to change the present before it gets any worse. And we're not just trying to influence adults, but also our peers, who might not realize that we are inheriting the world.

When thirty-nine students were granted the opportunity to let their voices be heard, we found out that there wasn't just one common voice; instead, the book turned into a compilation of many individuals each voicing a unique perspective. For that reason, we created a theme for this book where each piece has a "voice"—a voice of concern, a voice of hate, a voice of survival, awareness, hope, love, and many more. Each author chose his or her voice, and it represents what the writer wants to express in his or her writing, or what they believe it represents.

Some of us chose to write about how to achieve peace, while many more of us chose to write about violence. We all go to school in an area where violence is an inescapable part of life, one we are often forced to experience personally. We don't just see it on TV—we witness violence, and are often cast into the middle of it. We know firsthand that it's a brutal reality. And for that reason, we feel that we are qualified to speak about it.

We hope that through this book the world can see how we perceive the spectrum between violence and peace. And how it has affected us and influenced our way of life.

CONTENTS

THE NEXT GENERATION

by Nivia Brown

When people ask the question, "How do we achieve peace in a violent world?" I look into the faces of the young, point to them, and say, "Through you." When you finish reading this piece, I want you to know that not all young people *just live* in this world. Some of us are actually thinking about what goes on around us: We're thinking about the violence that occurs in our communities, and the things that happen to other youth all over the world. I think that world change depends on the younger children, sitting in kindergarten classes and learning how to count and to read. They are the ones who will redeem us, and they are the ones who hold the key to sustaining life.

My little sister is eleven years old. She is the queen of her world, and I respect her deeply for it. She has been able to create this wisdom-filled view of the world, and the way that it's "supposed" to be. She knows that the wars we fight have deeper meanings, and that the people we claim to be "evil" or "dangerous for our safety as Americans" are real human beings, not just villains who live in dark caves. She understands complex reasons for the black community's creation of the Black

Panther party and what the Black Panthers actually did. She knows why our young black brothas stand on the street corners after dark, hustlin' for a life that will only bring them death.

My sister's understanding is what makes me second-guess, and reassess, everything that I do. She looks up to me, and pressures me to stay on the right path. She empowers me in a way that even she doesn't understand, which makes me feel I owe her more and more every day. She gives new meaning to the phrase: "Each one, teach one." One of the main reasons I resist, speak up, and think critically is that I know she's the one who will have to deal with the garbage my generation leaves behind. I want her to be safe and sheltered long enough to develop her mind and spirit, and to be strong enough that no one can break her down. She's so young and so vulnerable; at the same time she is one of the strongest young women I know.

But as strong as my sister is, when we sit in front of the "idiot box," I watch this youthful and strong-willed young woman go from highly educated to highly vegetated. She opens her mind and all the negative views about women, people of color, and urban youth latch onto it, slowly destroy the powerful image she had of the world. The media is a scary thing, and I know that I don't have control over it. She watches it, and doesn't realize that, with every second that goes by, this "evil" propaganda enters her mind and slowly infects her subconscious.

I am not the type of person to present a bunch of bad situations and offer no solutions. One of the main things, I think, that can keep young people from losing all sense of self is education. When I say education, I mean teaching them more than math, science, and how Columbus discovered America. Teach them about something other than slavery and the Holocaust. Make it so that each and every student gets excited about school, so that they all get excited about getting a good and sturdy education. This is my wish for the world, and all the youth in it. I want to be able to walk into a classroom, sit in a chair, and know that, for the next hour and a half, I'm going to learn about something that relates to my community and me. I want to learn how to create a next-generation Black Panther Party or Brown Berets. I want to learn, in depth, about the resistance of the slaves in Haiti, how they led the world's only successful slave revolt, and how they created the first black republic. I want to learn about the resistance groups in Asia, how they fought against the powers that were, and whether they succeeded or not. I want to help plant the seed in the next generation of young people. I want them to know that they need to be complex thinkers and powerful fighters. I can't wait to grow up and live in this crazy world, so that I can change it. I know that I won't be alone—there's a whole army of us waiting to learn how to better use our insurgent minds to change the world. The revolution will not be televised, so stay tuned.

MENTAL REVOLUTIONS

by Michael Jordan

A man cuts in front of him in line. At first he looks dumbfounded, *Did that just happen...?* He starts to tremble as anxiety swells inside him. It happens all the time, even for the most insignificant reasons, but he can't stop it. From the pit of his stomach, up through his chest, the growing anxiety overtakes his mind. *The audacity ... what a jerk, who does he think he is? I should show him a thing or two; I can't wait in this line anymore....* The wake of his anxious anger leaves his muscles tight. He has a realization. *Oh my God, what am I doing...?* He looks at his clenched fists, takes a deep breath, and counts 3... 2... 1... He says, "Excuse me sir, but you cut the line." The man apologizes, not realizing what he has done, and goes to the end of the line. Another disaster thwarted by free will!

Humans are not bound to hateful paths. We know right from wrong. An eye for an eye is not the path to peace. We know this, but we rarely step away from it. This is true on any scale—from the American family to the poorest country in the world. We aren't born gun-toting cowboys; we are intelligent, thoughtful, free-thinking human beings. It's time we acted like it.

Stop trying to growl. You're a human being...
Human beings are different from animals because of choice, or, in other words, free will, or freedom of thought. Animals are driven by instincts alone. For everything they encounter, they have predisposed reactions. Even for new experiences, they work from their existing scope of reactions. They can run away, fight, explore, or do whatever is triggered. They react with the instincts that have perpetuated their species for generations. It is a rigid system wherein only those with the right impulses will live on. They are guided by instincts and predisposed reactions; this is not free will.

Humans, on the other hand, are physically designed for free will. This is evident in the presence of the frontal lobe, which is responsible for things like behavior and judgment. Our frontal lobes are bigger than those found in animals, giving us room to develop better mental capabilities. We are given the ability to control our emotional responses. Every time we are faced with a decision, we can make a new reaction (fresh, and never canned). Our responses *seem* to be repetitive reactions because we use past experiences and tailor our reactions to what we believe worked or didn't work. However, even though we are designed for free thought, it doesn't work seamlessly for everybody. We all have something dulling the brilliance of our free thought.

What's all that—moving away from home?
No, it's just my emotional baggage...
So what went wrong? Surprisingly, one answer can be found in the gentle whispers of a mother to her child, "Don't cry, don't cry, go to sleep." This sounds innocent enough, but it is only the beginning of the perpetual act of shoveling distress inside. We are conditioned from birth to force aside distressing situations inside ourselves. Virtually every human being has some type of repressed distress that in some way, consciously or not, is stashed away. The person who appears at peace with the world is not perfect; he or she just has less emotional baggage than the rest of us.

What is this emotional baggage, anyway? Well, it is the repression of any distressing event that muddles up our clear thinking. For a child, getting hurt, lost, or scared are monumental events. Any of these events hurt, and, naturally, a child cries. However, we see a young person cry, and our first idea is to say, "It's OK, it's OK, don't cry," or even, "Shut up or I'll give you something to really cry about!" The latter seems to hurt more, but they both have effects. We fail to realize that the child needs to cry. A child wants to cry and wants to know that someone is showing some kind of interest. Crying is the only way babies express grief. They may cry for a long time, but eventually they will get over it. This doesn't seem practical to a parent. Not only is it a lot of noise, but what are you supposed to do when you are in public? It is pretty annoying to other people, but isn't that the point? The baby shows distress and needs care, but we naturally try to shut it up. It doesn't exactly fit into our culture, because we take care of ourselves, and refuse to take responsibility for others. We don't want to bother anyone else, and want no one to bother us. Both cases perpetuate the smothering of expression.

The girls and the guys...
Everybody is vulnerable to distress in the world. There's nothing you can do but handle it as well as you can. Men are hindered, though, because society sets a double standard for men and women. It is considered acceptable for women to be emotional and, as a result, repress less than men. Men are not allowed to be emotional; they are taught differently. They have a distorted view of what it really means to be a "man." They may think that being a man is having stone-cold emotions, dominating people (especially women), and losing any sign of "femininity." To do this, a man has to be unwavering in his demeanor, and not cry over anything. The only possible exception would be in mourning someone's death. To meet the manly expectations requires massive amounts of repression. Guys try to get their grief out, but the only acceptable way they see to do this is simply

telling the story of what happened. This isn't always enough. This is not a true man. A "real man" is trustworthy, and knows he has responsibility for himself and those around him. He doesn't abuse himself or anyone else in any way. He takes responsibility for the physical, mental, emotional, and spiritual well-being of himself and those around him. He is sensitive; he gives support to and receives it from fellow humans, with love. This doesn't necessarily mean that guys have to go crying all the time, but they need to be aware, think clearly, and express their tribulations. If there were more "real men" around, it wouldn't be embarrassing or "girly" (a man's worst fear). Taking care of yourself and others is not girly; it is exactly what we need. The whole idea of gender roles is flawed anyway. In today's society men and women are more equal than ever. There shouldn't even be a reference to being a *real man*, or *real woman*. We should value being a *real human being*.

Going in circles...
When there is a distressing situation that isn't fully resolved, there is a smudge left on the thinking of that person. The more severe the distress, the bigger the smudge. When people get smudges on their minds, they don't think as clearly. The memories of the past smudges can be triggered, and the person becomes distressed again and cannot think clearly. Then another smudge will appear on their mind, and *it* is unlikely to be resolved. This becomes a cyclical experience, leading to more smudges, and more irrational thoughts.

This circle of mismanaged distress oscillates through people. This is evident in the Israeli/Palestinian conflict. There are decades of hard feelings, and nobody shows signs of forgiving or quitting. The Israelis bear down on the Palestinians with military dominance because the Palestinians keep sending suicide bombers, and vice versa. It is a vicious circle that gets harder and harder to break as more lives are taken. It has escalated from a land take-over, to eye-for-an-eye slayings. But it is more than just a simple circle. In the midst of the conflict are people who just want to live their lives, but get caught in the crossfire and pulled into the conflict.

On any scale, these circles of distress can thrive. It's hard to scrub off all of the smudges that have been built up by past suffering. If anything, we can only hope to help the next generation hold true to what it is to be a real human being.

Livin' smudge-free

We know what we have to change, so the next obvious step is to take action. To live this smudge-free life, we have to find outlets for our distress. The simplest ways to vent distress can be crying, screaming, or just talking to someone. If you don't like talking to anybody you know, or don't have anyone you can trust, there are plenty of resources, like counselors (including spiritual ones, such as priests) and anonymous phone-support groups. Getting a distressful event off of your chest and freeing your mind can also be done through other forms of expression. For example, you could write a poem, start a diary, sing, paint, or anything that provides a medium for getting a message across. Humanity is going to forever be caught in the smudgy circle unless we take steps toward resolution. We need to take a deep breath, and begin to use what rational thought we have left to mend the past and protect the future.

A STEP TOWARD
MAKING A DIFFERENCE

by Courtney King

When I was two, my parents got a divorce. I was too young to understand what that meant; all I knew was that Daddy wasn't around much. A few years later, my mother, my sister, and I moved into the Potrero Hill projects in San Francisco, where my mother came to experience it all. She feared the gunshots at night, worked two jobs to provide food and clothing for her family, and struggled with the result of a divorce that forced her to raise a family of two girls on her own. My sister attended Lowell High School at the time, and I was in elementary school. When my parents divorced, my mother could not afford a house, or even a decent apartment, in which to raise her family. The last thing she wanted to do was move into public housing and put her children in those conditions. But there was no other option. This hurt her very much. Through prayer, my mother eased her pain and stress. She made it through the tough times and is now stronger and wiser.

Because of this experience, my mother has always wanted the best for my sister and me. She wants us to be happy, educated young black women. To her, the best thing in life is an education, because she did not attend a four-year university. She migrated to California from Mississippi (following my father), looking for a better opportunity in life. Instead, it led her to instability, because things did not turn out right with my father. She now looks at it all as a huge mistake, and wishes she had known better.

As a young African-American woman getting ready to graduate from high school, I see why my mother worries and wants the best for my sister and me. I now see how life is hard for minorities, and women of color. California was once a dreamland for people of all nationalities who wanted to succeed in life. But it's not easy to succeed without a job or an education. Many minorities living in California suffer from budget cuts, unemployment, poverty, and violence within communities, and we don't have the money to live as comfortably as we would like.

In San Francisco, the communities that suffer the most are the low-income minority communities like Hunters Point, Potrero Hill, and Sunnydale. What worries me is that I have not seen much change in Black communities in my lifetime. African-American males are still killing each other, making the homicide count in San Francisco too high. What can you look forward to in life when all you see is a continuous cycle of violence in your community?

When I was nine, my sister, who I looked up to as a second mother, went off to college at San Diego State University. At that time, things became hard for my mother, which led me at a young age to feel unstable at home. I moved in with my father and we now live in Hunters Point. We may live in a better part of the neighborhood, but what surrounds us are areas that have been forgotten over time.

When I stand outside on our deck, I view the beautiful San Francisco Bay and the Bay Bridge. But if I look closely and deeply beneath me and beyond, I can see the poor condition that Hunters Point is in. I often hear gunshots at night, and wake up hearing about the latest deaths in my community. What I fear is not making it home one day because of a shooting on my bus. Many people have lost loved ones from guns, but no one knows or understands why young African-American men are killing each other. Not only is the violence in the community a problem, but the condition of the community is a problem, too. Hunters Point suffers from pollution because of landfills in the area. The people of Hunters Point have been exposed to chemicals that cause birth defects, asthma, breast cancer, and lymphoma. These chemicals are from a power plant that has not been moved, although it's affecting the lives of the African-American population. I feel many African-American people have lost faith in America because of the conditions in which we're put, and how we're ignored when it comes to issues of health and safety from violence.

My way to deal with my environment is to keep myself from getting caught up in the cycle of violence in my neighborhood. I do this by going to school, and keeping up my grades. I also work as a Peer Health Educator to further my education in the health field. I cofacilitate a girls' group here at my school, where we talk about topics like pregnancy prevention, sexually transmitted infections, birth control methods, awareness of lesbian, bisexual, gay, transgender, and queer identities, relationships, and body image. By being a Peer Health Educator, I know I'm giving back to my community and educating young women to make a difference in their lives.

Education is the key to success, and without it life in America is hard. In order for me to make it in life, I must go to college. As a minority, what worries me is that college is expensive, and this deters many blacks from attending. Some of us are stuck in these poor communities and in the cycle of violence because we lack money to enter college or to make something of ourselves.

Now living in Pacifica, my mother looks back at what she experienced and saw in her community. What struck her the most were the young African-American men killing each other and not sticking around to be fathers to their children. It also saddens her to see women of color put into situations that are hopeless because of the lack of money and education. She has decided to give back to her community by providing foster care for young African-American boys in need of a home. She wants to make a difference in their lives, so they won't become part of the cycle of violence, and so that they can grow up to be responsible and educated young men. My mother learned from her past experience that without an education, it's hard to make something of yourself. She is determined to help as many people as possible, including my sister, her foster children, and me. She will do this by motivation. Even though she was not fortunate enough to have a formal education, she will make a difference in this world.

GOVERNMENT OF HYPOCRITES
=
STREETS OF VIOLENCE

by Ben Schuttish

In America, many people think that violence is the only way to resolve conflict. Violence has become more than just wartime battles; it has become a way of life for American people. Although it appears that they're model citizens—smart men and women, supposedly the smartest in the country—who understand that violence is not the answer, our leaders are doing the exact same thing that gang members in cities all over the United States are doing. While the U.S. government is sending thousands of troops to risk their lives in the war in Iraq, people here are waging war on each other, killing each other in the streets of cities in the U.S. They are turning to violence immediately, instead of as a final option, as it should be. Violence has become the main, first reaction that people take toward their problems.

I can understand how solving conflict with violence would be the first instinct to humans. Many times, when I am involved in a conflict with an outside force, I want to solve the problem through fighting. Most people do. Many times throughout my life, I have seen a person become provoked and then act on the natural impulse to fight. Deep inside every person's soul is a temper; this temper may be either big or small. Being confronted or provoked incites natural rises in the levels of the temper. A hot temper overcomes people's good sense, and makes them to want to fight back. This never solves their real problems, though. It may make them feel good at the moment, but later on they all say that they regret fighting, because it caused more problems for them down the line. It takes a stronger person to use self-control and resist his or her natural impulses for violence. It takes a smarter person to realize that using violence to solve problems is not the only way, or the best way. If I am contemplating becoming involved in a fight, I would have everything to lose, and nothing to gain, in the long run. The momentary satisfaction is not worth the problems that last even longer.

The world is stuck in a hurricane of violence and war. People are killing each other in gang wars in the cities, countries are attacking each other based only on suspicions, and policemen are beating and killing innocent people just because of their misguided beliefs about racial profiling. How can the U.S. government expect civilians to not take part in violence when it is acting violently itself? If government officials really want violence to come to an end in urban streets, as they say, then they need to set that example themselves, and try to lead the world out of the neverending spiral of war and violence that we are involved in. The U.S. government is being run by hypocrites who preach peace to citizens, and then inflict violence and warfare on other countries with no real proof or reason for doing so.

Because of the long history of wars that America has been involved in (Civil War, WWI, WWII, Korean War, Vietnam War, etc.), many Americans believe that there is no other way to resolve conflict. They learn it, when they are young, from their parents and other adults in their lives. President George W. Bush learned it from his father when his father was president, and now he is taking what he learned and applying it to the war in Iraq. President Bush is putting millions of people's lives on the line because of a suspicion about weapons of mass destruction in that country. Instead of immediately declaring war, President Bush should have used his brain to think of some other options first. He couldn't help it, though, because war was what he had been taught by his father. This is wrong. War should be based upon more than just suspicions. The United States, being the most powerful nation in the world, should not overuse its power against smaller, weaker countries such as Iraq. The U.S. shouldn't ever declare war. The only way that the U.S. should engage in battle should be if they are attacked, or if another country declares war on the U.S.

I am not saying that war should never be an option, but it should be the last resort. Sometimes there are situations where there are no other ways out of a conflict, and a war must happen. However, authority figures cannot expect people to turn away from violence when the U.S. government, which is supposed to be the example for the rest of the population, does exactly what it tells everyone else not to do. I can't look up to the members of the U.S. government, because they are hypocrites. People in America should not look at this administration's officials as examples of what to do when conflict arises, because they have proven that while they say all the right things, they do the opposite. Until we get a government in place that says—and *does*—the correct things with regard to war and conflict, there will always be violence on the streets of cities in the United States of America.

LETTER TO MOM

by Shirley Chen

Dear Mom,
 I don't think I will ever be strong enough to say this to your face, or at least not now. So I think writing this will be easier, and will come out better. What I am writing to you about has never gone well in conversations between us. It's been always shaky, and it seems to come up so few times that I can count them on my fingers. I never knew if it would hurt you, or make you think of the past, if I were to mention it or talk about it. It seems so clear that you just want to move on; maybe it just seems like that to me. But, I want to know, so let me ask bluntly: How did Dad's death affect you? I have all these feelings and thoughts inside me, and because of what happened to him, I worry and wonder a lot about you. What happened affected me deeply and I want to share those feelings with you.

 He died when I was so young, only three years old, and I didn't have many feelings that I can remember. I just knew that he was gone, though I didn't understand why. But as I grew up, I started to understand, and I experienced some feelings, deep inside, that I wish I didn't have. I felt so alone, at times. I never really wanted to talk to Willy about this. He was just going to act like his usual brotherly self and say, "Leave me alone, I don't want to talk about it," or at least I was scared he would say that. I was frightened to talk to anybody about it, and to be honest, I am still kind of scared writing this to you. I just hope you understand what I am trying to say to you. I hope you take it in, because I feel so unheard by you sometimes. I don't really understand these feelings I have, either, so if you get confused, let me begin by saying that I feel a bit confused too.

Because of his death, I have developed concerns and worries that constantly run through my head. I worry about you and Willy every day. You have always wondered why I worry so much and why I can't just let things be sometimes. The reason is that I don't want what happened to Dad to happen to you, Willy, or the people I love. I am scared of what might happen in the world in which we live. I know people are going to die from violence, but I don't want you to be one of them. Dad was shot in his store, and I don't want that to happen to you, or Willy. You work only a few blocks from my school, and it makes me feel slightly better because I know I can get to you in a few minutes if you ever need me. But it's not the safest neighborhood; that's why I call every few hours to make sure you're where you're supposed to be. I know you're busy at four in the afternoon, but I'd rather bother you for a minute than worry about you for the rest of the day. I know it's a bit selfish, but your safety is always on my mind.

I know I shouldn't worry so much, but violence came into our family and it has affected me so deeply. And it's so hard not to worry—because of all those crazy situations that happen on television, which constantly remind me of what happened to our family. I know I shouldn't let the media influence me, but it does, just like it does millions of people in the world. Just the other day, on the news, there was a story about a mother and daughter who were battered to death by some random man who still hasn't been caught. Even though it happened in Fremont, and not in our city, it scares me that there are crazy people out there. I try to keep in mind that it doesn't happen every day and it's unusual. But the problem is that it seems normal.

I have felt the pain of losing someone, and I don't want to experience it again. I will never feel Dad's touch again, or see his smile, hold his hand and walk with him down the street, hear him speak, learn from him—all those things a daughter gets to do with her father. I will never again be able to sit with him and look at the pictures of me sitting on the counter of his store, with his arms around me. I have lost those moments with him forever, and I don't want to lose any moments with you. I want all the things a daughter gets to do with her mother as the years pass. I know now that every minute I spend with you is precious. I don't want you to die violently too. I know this seems dramatic, but these are the thoughts that run through my head constantly.

We don't live in the safest city, or in the safest areas either. In these neighborhoods, violence is often used as a way to solve problems easily. I am scared that you are going to get caught in the middle of one of these violent acts. I know you also worry about me a lot. You think I will be taken advantage of, because of the type of person I am. But you don't have to worry about that. I have led my life a certain way, and have learned how to handle conflicts, because of what you have taught me and because of what happened to Dad. I live my life carefully, not to step on any toes. I am constantly aware of what could happen, and the possibility of violence around me. I am nice, and I try to be a kind person, because I don't want to have discord with people. I want to use peace instead of violence as a solution.

I wish people would see that violence not only affects and influences people who are closely involved, but it also affects their families, friends, their community, and the world. None of us, including me, know the murderer of my father, but he has caused us pain that will never disappear. This killer is a stranger to me, but he has left a big hole in my heart where my father's love would be. He did this without laying a finger on me. What he did not only ended my father's life, but affected everybody who loved and cared for him.

Violence spreads like a deadly disease, because it gets into people's minds and becomes familiar to them. It doesn't seem as dangerous anymore because it is so common. It's shown as a solution to younger generations, and it then continues to trickle down into future generations. That belief spreads when people talk about it, when the media shows it, when role models flaunt it, and when the entertainment industry emphasizes it. People become numb to it and they treat it as though it's normal for everyday life when it should not be normal at all. Violence is not normal! It is not a solution and if it has to be used in self-defense, it should be the last resort. I am glad that you taught me that fact, and you have taught me to understand and to remember it well. Now I can spread that knowledge to the people around me.

But even though I try not to have conflicts, I am not perfect. I have had clashes with people. I solved them through communication and by making compromises—like you always told me to do when I bickered with Willy. The saying "Mother knows best" seems to be true so many times a day. Willy and I do get along better; that's why I know to follow your advice in my everyday life. And at the age of seventeen, my disputes with others have not evolved into any violent situations, and I've never had to deal with violence personally. In my mind, I think I will know what to do if I have to. But, I truly believe in my heart that it will never get that far, because I won't let it happen.

I know that the world, and people, are not perfect. The only way to achieve a peaceful world is to practice peace, and to affect the lives of others by setting good examples for the present generation. Thank you, Mom, for doing that for me. I have learned so much from you, and I hope that every time we do talk, as time goes by, you will teach me more.

Love always,
Shirley

YOU LED ME TO BELIEVE

by Erica Barajas

It's hard for me to distinguish reality from fiction
because of the nightmares you made me live.

I know they're real because of all the physical
      marks
you left on my body.

I was blinded by love.
You took advantage of my disability
and attacked with no remorse.

After a while I stopped feeling pain.

It became a daily routine.
I woke up,
ate,
got beat, and slept.

You led me to believe that a simple kiss
    from your lips
could make up for the moment I was in
    the corner covering my face.

At first I tried to fight it.

As soon as you raised your hand
I was quick to ball up my fist and respond
but you overpowered me with such force
that couldn't be tamed.

ANOTHER DAY

by Alicia Torres

It was a sunny afternoon at 12:30, and school had ended early because of finals week. Robin, a sixteen-year-old who never does his homework but always knows what he is talking about, usually hangs out with Snara, a confused seventeen-year-old student who has so much to say but is always unsure. After class, they both decided to stay and talk to their history teacher, Ms. Prain, about questions they had about what was going on in the world today.

"What are you interested in knowing?" asked Ms. Prain. "What brings you here?"

"I was interested in knowing how imperialism started," Snara said with a curious face, rushing the words out of her mouth. "Lately, I've been thinking a lot about Manifest Destiny and how the U.S. accomplished it. And as the country expanded it never seemed satisfied, because it wanted to conquer Asia and the Pacific. After I thought about all that, I was thinking about the Spanish-American War and how wrong that was. The imperialism that went on in the Boxer Rebellion in 1900 was wrong. The British controlling India was unfair. The British controlling the thirteen colonies wasn't just. The

U.S. intervention in Latin America was also imperialism. Even the war in Iraq is imperialist. It's got to be!"

"Calm down, Snara," Robin said with a big smile on his face. "It's not the end of the world. Or is it?" Robin turned to Ms. Prain and calmly said, "She wants to discuss the war in Iraq."

"I see… What is bothering you?" said Ms. Prain, who sat at her desk, waving her pencil around.

"Nothing's bothering me. It's just that… well, yeah, basically I want to discuss the word 'imperialism' and the war in Iraq. I don't agree with the war, because I think the president started a war that should have never been started," said Snara.

"Why do you believe this war is wrong?" asked Ms. Prain.

"I didn't agree with Congress giving the president power to declare the war on Iraq. Congress wasn't thinking. From that moment on, Bush made this war his war," said Snara.

"That's true," Robin said, agreeing with Snara. "This war is completely unfair because Bush based this war on weapons that were never found to this day, and a so-called 'threat' from Iraq that goes back eleven years."

"Clear that up for me. What happened eleven years ago?" asked Ms. Prain, winking and moving her hair back.

"Eleven years ago, after the Persian Gulf War, the U.S. put conditions on the Iraqi regime," said Snara. "The conditions required Iraq to destroy its weapons of mass destruction, discontinue its development of weapons, and to stop the Iraqi regime's support of terrorist groups. The U.N. Security Council imposed economic sanctions on Iraq, and that made the people in Iraq poorer. I just don't get it. And now we want to reconstruct Iraq, when a few years ago we were hurting their economic status."

"The Iraqi ambassador to the United Nations made a statement to the Security Council that Iraq had no intention of attacking anyone now or in the future with any weapons," said Robin.

Just then, Joaner, a student in the same class, walked in. She had been listening to the whole conversation outside of the cracked door and decided to step into the conversation. Joaner walked with a very straight posture toward Robin and said, "Of course the ambassador would say that, wouldn't he?"

"Hey, Joaner," Snara said, smiling at Joaner's short stature.

"Nice to see you joining us, Joaner," said Ms. Prain. "Next time warn us that you're listening."

"Hey, hear me out," said Robin, getting frustrated. "President Bush still pushed this war. He doesn't see that there could be peace without war. He is simply a war president who's making bad decisions. I don't know why he's in office anyway. What were the American voters thinking? This so-called reconstruction of Iraq is just costing us too many of our soldiers' lives."

"So Joaner, do you believe imperialism is going on in this conflict with Iraq?" continued Ms. Prain.

"Let me answer first," Snara said. "Yes, it is. It falls back on imperialism. President Bush is trying to take control of Iraq. I personally think money is involved, along with oil, and it's about having the power of more territory. Or it could be about getting re-elected."

"I believe helping Iraq is a good thing," said Joaner, slowly moving her hand to her smooth-skinned face. "The people in that country must be helped. Saddam Hussein needed to be overthrown. He wasn't doing anything good for those people. It was about time someone interfered. I believe the U.S. did the right thing. The war in Iraq was also necessary to stop terrorism and send a message that the United States isn't a place you can mess with. I agree with it all."

"How can you justify the war in Iraq? Tell me," Snara said as she directly looked at Joaner's eyes. "President Bush based the attack on Iraq over weapons of mass destruction that were never found. They were not a threat to us. It was all bullshit."

"What about the U.S. soldiers?" Robin added. "Did you ever consider how they are risking their lives? Do the soldiers seem to think that violence is another way to solve Iraq's problems? Most of those soldiers *are* ignorant enough to agree on a false war that should never have been started."

"Hey, hold on. Most soldiers do agree with the war," Snara said. "But I got a friend in the Army that doesn't agree with the war in Iraq or the reconstruction. But he's the only soldier I have ever heard that doesn't agree with it."

"They are fighting for their beliefs, which are the right ones," Joaner said with an assured face. "People just don't see how much their help will change many people's lives."

"Think about how the people in Iraq feel," said Snara, looking at everyone in the room. "Yeah, the U.S. government got rid of Saddam Hussein, but our soldiers are invading their country by being in Iraq."

"Our soldiers are in a foreign country and they're setting up rules for the Iraqis," Robin said as he pulled up his dark blue jeans, which were falling off. "Joaner, I just want you to see how the U.S. is using its power to take advantage of other countries. You can't tell me that the U.S. isn't taking over Iraq and isn't indirectly gaining control of the political or economic life of Iraq."

"Yes it is, but it's for the good of the people," said Joaner.

"I'm right, though. Imperialism *is* what is going on!" said Robin, looking directly at Joaner.

"What's wrong with imperialism? If that's the case, then imperialism can be a positive thing. Imperialism in Iraq is a benefit to the people who live there," Joaner said, as she smiled, because she was happy she had flipped the conversation.

"Imperialism isn't a positive thing! Taking over another country for your own benefit isn't anywhere near positive," Snara added, more frustrated than earlier. "Don't you get it, Joaner?"

"You know what I get? This issue of Iraq has split our country in two," Joaner said, and she frowned. "The people who agree with Bush and the war in Iraq and the people who don't. One thing I believe is that both beliefs are different ways to find peace. Americans want to stop terrorism, because we want peace. Americans want to stop the war in Iraq, because we want to stop the violence between American soldiers and the former Iraqi regime. Americans want to stop the reconstruction in Iraq because we want to stop the violence between American soldiers and Iraqi citizens. We all want peace, it's just that everyone has different ways to get there."

"I agree with that," said Snara, as she removed some of her wild hair from her face, and smiled.

"Most definitely, I agree," Robin said as he took a deep breath from the intense conversation. "Peace is all that any of us want. The violence hopefully will end soon."

"I'm glad I could provide a room where you could all argue and finally agree," Ms. Prain said, and then laughed.

"Let's all go get something to eat, I'm hungry," Snara said. "I'm looking too cute to be indoors arguing with y'all."

"Yeah, let's go," Robin said as he grabbed his backpack.

"Whatever, I'm hungry too," Joaner added as they all walked out of the classroom.

"Hey, I still think the war in Iraq and reconstruction is totally unfair!" Snara said, closing the door of Ms. Prain's room. She grinned with satisfaction because she'd gotten the last word.

AT WHAT AGE?

by Maurice Dwight Hightower

Without our past, there can be no future.

[Note: The following is an article from the *San Francisco Bay View* newspaper published on October 16, 2002, reprinted here, in its entirety, courtesy of the author, Lee Hubbard.] —M.D.H.

60 BATON-WIELDING POLICE HIT, TRAUMATIZE THURGOOD MARSHALL STUDENTS

San Francisco—A student fistfight escalated into a violent confrontation with police at Thurgood Marshall Academic High School in the Bayview district Friday. Over 60 police officers came into the school wielding batons, hitting and traumatizing students.

"School should be the place for a safe environment," said Channing Hale, a sophomore at the school. "But today, it felt like we were on the streets."

In a press conference later that day, Jackie Wright, a spokesperson for the San Francisco Unified School District, called the incident "an altercation that got out of hand."

Wright stressed that no weapons were involved amongst the students. She also contended there was no violence at the school, but that assessment differs from the accounts of students and teachers at the scene.

Channing Hale said the police hit her with a baton as she was standing in the hallway, trying to get around the fight on her way to class. "I was told to move by an officer, and then I was hit in the face," said Hale. She said she fell to the ground after being struck.

Franchischa Maufas, another

student at Marshall, said she was hit in the chest and slapped with a stick while walking from one class to another. "The police were all on one of my friends, my home girl," said Maufas. "When I told the officer to stop, I got hit by a stick."

Michael Puccinelli, police captain at the Bayview Station, said that police had to respond in full force. "There was a riot going on in that school," he said. "If we do nothing, we are derelict in our duty and someone might get killed in there."

Puccinelli said that the police were forced to act, because they were faced with an angry crowd of students, one of whom, he claimed, took a baton from an officer.

"We had to move the kids," said Puccinelli. "The kids were confrontational."

The police arrived at around 10:40 a.m. A fire alarm had sounded, bringing students out of their classrooms into the hallways and toward the schoolyard, as they are taught to do at the sound of the alarm.

One of the most disturbing allegations to come out of the incident was the report of a police officer brandishing a firearm and threatening a student in the middle of the hallway.

"We were coming out of the office as the fight was going on, and an officer took his gun out at one of the students and told him, 'Don't make me use this,'" said Ely Guolio, a student at the school. "I was shocked."

Police arrested two students and a teacher, 29-year-old Anthony Peebles, a literature teacher at the school, who was charged with battery on an officer,

interfering with an arrest, and suspicion of inciting a riot.

Peebles said he was in his classroom when he heard a lot of noise in the hallway. "I went outside and I saw all of these police with students handcuffed and I wanted to know what was going on," said Peebles. "I walked into the office and I then saw a girl student thrown out of the door by the police face first."

He went back to his room and got a video camera to record what was happening in his school. Police seized the camera when they arrested Peebles.

'The police handled this situation ridiculously," he said.

"This has been a clear and blatant example of irresponsible decisions by the administrators and the police that resulted in this conflict that escalated," said Jose Luis Pavan of Youth Making a Change, a program of Coleman Advocates. "It is a case of clear and brutal force focused on African American youth by the San Francisco Police Department."

Opened in 1994, Thurgood Marshall is a rigorous academic high school with 1,100 students at a site off Silver Avenue once home to Pelton Middle School and later to Phillip and Sala Burton Academic High School. A college preparatory school with a focus on science, mathematics, and technology, Marshall was intended as an alternative to the popular and prestigious Lowell High School, one of the nation's top performing schools. According to the school district, Marshall boasts a 92 percent graduation rate and average daily attendance.

"This was like our Lowell," a parent told the Examiner. "We had more students going to (UC) Berkeley than anywhere in the district."

Students cited a lack of school discipline, lack of school spirit, and administrators who do not try to develop relationships with the students as common concerns since new administrators took over the school this year.

"People see a school like Thurgood Marshall and they feel it is a school that doesn't deserve to be treated like Lowell," said Nivia Brown, a sophomore at Marshall. "It is sad, because there are students here who used to be successful, but it seems we are faced with different issues every day from the school officials and other people who should be helping us the most."

They say something as little as a fist can win a war, but they never say something as little or as simple as a phone call can begin one. Throughout history, many great minds have had their words manipulated and their images categorized. These people are the few who think outside of the box—those who would rather enhance their individuality than conform to the majority. They are the TRUE MINORITIES. As children, we are taught to accept loss, but to lose has been the equivalent of failure. Therefore we are expected to win "by any means necessary." A simple phrase such as this has complex meanings and, when misinterpreted, paves the way for ignorance.

"Great minds influence life. Ignorant minds hinder (destroy) life."

—Maurice Hightower

These are the actions that took place at Thurgood Marshall Academic High School on October 11, 2002. Influencing many; seen through the eyes of one.

Breathe ... Breathe ... I want to calm myself, but the anger, the pain that has been injected into my blood has altered—mutated—my heartbeat into something unknown.

My eyes open. Tears of anger soak back into my sight, rising from the ground like the many souls lost from my generation.

I'm walking backward. The door closes in front of me, then opens, welcomes me, but reverse is the only way.

!!KKKKCCCUUF. Air, my voice, is sucked back into my mouth, filling my lungs with the sickness of an oppressed life. My body plays pinball against the walls, step-by-step down the stairs.

Down the stairs, only seeing what's ahead. Knowing what's behind, but being pulled by the past, back into it.

My shirt zips up in various places as the stitching and the fabric pull it together. The ripped and torn shirt was once new and has replenished itself before my eyes.

The door opens to hell and it seems as if I moon-walked into the depths of fear.

AHHH!! My eardrums vibrate as the sound of YOUTH pulls itself out of my head and back into the mouths of many.

Pain surrounds me; rage fills me.

I watch as children's voices are broken and their dreams are crushed by wood, metal, skin, and bone by those who are here to "SERVE AND PROTECT."

The sound of wood and bone interacting with each other makes a distinct noise as his nightstick rises from my arm, through the air, and back to his side.

We are walking forward now as THEY ARE RETREATING back to their many cars.

They shift into reverse and vanish into the mist, leaving behind only the fading sound of sirens.

In front of the school I'm now standing, shoulder-to-shoulder with what seems to be an endless line of students.

Our heads tilted to the sky, ears chasing the sound of screams, eyes searching for something only fate would find.

Ignorant to the fact that our ears were chasing ourselves, through time … in the soon-to-be future.

The clouds begin to open up and the sunlight enters through our pores and fills us with life.

We are YOUTH again, filled with love, anger, strength, *mistakes*, but most of all, understanding.

We watch.

He rises from the ground like a puppet controlled by his master. His face expands from a transitory, deformed state, and overpowers the fist that was once engraved into it.

AT WHAT AGE is reality brought down upon a child's head and life exposed?

DARK SECRETS OF AMERICA

by Theresa Nguyen

Violence, violence, and more violence is what keeps on happening in the world today. From community affairs to world affairs, everyone is affected by violence. From gang-banging on a corner of the Tenderloin district in San Francisco, to the Iraq War, violence seems to be everywhere. But how is it right for the U.S. government to punish the people who use violence as a solution, when it is exactly the same solution the government uses?

In the streets of America, fights, gunshots, and drama break out every day, and approximately 2.1 million Americans are currently incarcerated for crimes that they have committed.[1] It is assumed that the U.S. government is the one who has the right to punish them. But how can the U.S. government put itself in that position, when it, too, has committed many criminal acts throughout the world? Throughout history, the U.S. government has committed many atrocities. Some even worse than the crimes that have been committed by the many felons incarcerated in U.S. prisons. From murder, to rapes, to assault and battery, theft, and even massacres, the U.S. government has been involved in these acts in more ways than one; yet they still decide to punish others for their crimes. Isn't that just a bit hypocritical?

One shocking example of the wrongdoings of the U.S. government was the senseless slaughter of 500 innocent Vietnamese citizens by the United States Army. In the village of My Lai lived 700 Vietnamese citizens. On March 16, 1968, American soldiers led by Lieutenant Calley went on a killing spree. In that one day, they exterminated almost three-quarters of the population of the village. The soldiers gathered all of the people left in the village (mostly women, children and elderly men) into a ditch, and opened fire. Anyone who was still alive was shot again until they were dead. As the soldiers mercilessly slaughtered civilians that they had tossed into the ditch, many mothers fell on top of their children to protect them from the gunshots. As they were being fired upon, they held their children tight, put their hands over the children's mouths, and told them not to move, not to speak—to act as if they were dead—or the shooting would never stop. Many of the women in My Lai were raped, brutally beaten, and tortured before their deaths. The few survivors would live to see the hundreds of bodies of their mutilated children, fathers, mothers, and neighbors scattered throughout the streets. What was supposed to be a hunt for Viet Cong soldiers turned out to be a massacre of hundreds of innocent victims.

This massacre would have been covered up if it hadn't been for a man named Ronald Ridenhour, who heard of the incident, and began an investigation of his own to see if it was really true. Finding out that this story was indeed true, he wrote a letter about what had happened in My Lai. He felt so strongly about this incident that he sent a copy of his letter to President Nixon, the Pentagon, and several Congressmen. He pushed them to do something about the incident, but it was not until a year or two later that action was taken.

But were these crimes ever truly punished? Because the American public had heard about what had happened in My Lai, through the many stories and pictures that were published, Calley, as well as many other U.S. officials involved in this brutal massacre, was put on trial. In the end only Calley was found guilty. Although 500 people were killed, Calley was charged only with the murder of thirty "Oriental human beings" at an intersection, the murder of seventy more in a ditch, shooting a man that held his hands up begging for his life, and killing a child who was running away. He was sentenced to lifetime imprisonment, but with the help of President Nixon, he ended up being let out on parole after serving only three years. Many Americans saw Calley as a scapegoat for what really happened in My Lai, and felt his sentence was unfair. To please the public, President Nixon ordered Calley to be put under house arrest. Hundreds of people lost their lives under Calley's command, but he served only three years in prison. Now, where was the justice in this?

Crimes are crimes, but what makes a government's crime different from a crime committed by an American citizen? Under the Nixon administration's leadership, Vietnam was a place full of death due to the bombs that were dropped by the U.S government. But, as always, the U.S government was not put on trial and charged for the millions of lives that were lost due to its actions. The example of My Lai, and the Vietnam War as a whole, shows that when the U.S. government is behind a crime that causes the deaths of thousands of people, it's okay, but when it's a crime that is committed by an ordinary citizen, it's not. Throughout history, the U.S. government has tried to cover up many of the horrible things that it has done to other people. The massacre of My Lai is just one of many examples of the horrific abuse that the U.S. has taken part in and even tried to hide from the public.

Even today, this cycle of violence has not ended. Since the war in Iraq began, thousands of Iraqi citizens, and 548 American citizens, have lost their lives to date. But for what? Many people are putting their lives at risk to find weapons of mass destruction that seem nonexistent. Innocent people are being killed left and right, and it seems as if the U.S government is responsible.

Murderers and rapists should not go unpunished, no matter what the circumstances. But if the U.S. government punishes people for their crimes, the government itself should be held accountable for the many crimes that it has committed, as well.

---

[1] www.prisonpolicy.org/articles/factsaboutcrime.pdf

WHERE I LIVE

by Adreena Winnfield

L et me take you on a tour of where I live. I live where it's hard to walk three blocks without seeing a memorial for someone shot and killed. Huge piles of flowers, teddy bears, pictures, balloons, candy, T-shirts, cards, and alcohol bottles are stacked toward the sky. There was one incident where a young man, nineteen years old, was gunned down right in front of my house. He was shot in broad daylight, and he later died. Another teenage boy was shot in the head, also in broad daylight. He was shot on Third Street in front of a Metro PC store. Of course there were plenty of witnesses in both cases, yet the murderers still walk the streets.

I live in San Francisco, California. But I bet this is not the tour you would expect. No, it's not the Golden Gate Bridge, Fisherman's Wharf, or a ride on the cable cars. This is Bayview/Hunters Point (BVHP). Where I live, violence is the way of life. It is not uncommon for a child eleven to eighteen years old to own a gun. Some children even carry other weapons like knives, bats, sticks, stun guns, and knock-out rings. The saddest thing is that kids bring these weapons to school every day, in fear of their lives. Most of them don't want to harm anyone, but they feel they need to protect themselves. It's a vicious cycle. I know boys who no longer catch the bus (MUNI) to school or home for fear of getting hurt. They either walk or get rides. They figure that if they got shot at on the MUNI they would have nowhere to run. If they're on foot, at least they have a chance to get away. I know other boys who take longer bus routes to get home to avoid riding in certain areas. (Instead of taking one bus, they catch two or three buses.) I know young men who cannot catch the MUNI to BVHP—they have to be in cars, for if certain people see them, they will not make it out of BVHP alive. When boys and girls walk around or go certain places, they have to watch their backs at all times. Some children in BVHP can't go to certain malls, movies, stores, restaurants, and even schools, for fear of their lives.

It's normal for me to hear police and ambulance sirens throughout the day and late into the night. It's okay to hear several rounds of gunshots and never hear or see the police, even though there's a police station right in back of my house. It's all right for men and women to stand in front of corner stores, selling and smoking drugs, and shooting craps for money.

But why is it okay for them to break the law, often right in front of the police? Why don't the police say anything? Every day, the officers walk or drive by, and they don't say a word. They are not blind! I truly believe that this behavior would not be tolerated in many other neighborhoods in San Francisco such as the Avenues, the Excelsior, the Richmond, the Sunset, Diamond Heights, or the Castro. So why is this behavior accepted in BVHP? Is it because this is what is expected of this neighborhood? Sometimes I think BVHP is expected to destroy itself. Why?

Where I live it is common to see fights in the street, on the bus, in schools, in front of grocery stores, at parties, and anywhere else you can imagine. Young girls think that it's "cute" to be in gangs and go around stealing from people and jumping other girls. Girls are jumped and severely beaten just for being in the wrong place at the wrong time.

There have been nights when I could not sleep, worrying about my safety and that of my loved ones. I would just lie awake at night asking God to protect me and all of the other youth in BVHP, and to stop the killings. I always picture someone close to me, or even myself, getting shot and killed. Other people have told me they also have dreams like this. Some wake up in pools of sweat.

So what can we do to stop the violence in BVHP? First, we, as a community, must start in our homes and schools. You, moms and dads, should wrap your children with love and care. Spend more time with your children, know your children's whereabouts. You should know who their friends are, with whom they hang. (Even though it may not seem important, it is. Youth have a lot of influence over each other.) You, teachers, should notify parents when students don't show up to class, or when they're not doing their work. Teachers should also show care and love toward their students, and let them know that they're important. Children need to be taught right from wrong, how to respect, and how to love others. They need to be taught that a life of guns, money, and drugs is not the type of life to aspire to. They should know that there is life beyond "The Point" and that education—or a casket—are the only ways out.

We need help from our mayor: you, Mr. Gavin Newsom. We need help from our governor: you, Mr. Arnold Schwarzenegger, to step up and speak out against the violence in BVHP. Not only to speak out but also to take action, to help BVHP stop the violence. We need the local law enforcement to work with us to stop the violence, secure our neighborhoods, solve the homicides, to be our friend and not our enemy.

The street memorials are heartbreaking. They are signs of black-on-black crime. They are letting us know how children are dying violently—younger and younger every day. Where I live, you're considered lucky if you live to see your eighteenth birthday. But we need these monuments. We need them to keep alive the memories of the loved ones lost. To let people know that our brothers, sisters, fathers, or boyfriends will never be forgotten. We need the monuments to let people know that we are ready to take steps to stop the violence in BVHP.

FROM POCKET-CHECK
TO REALITY CHECK

by Richard L Cheung

In my life so far I have been "pocket-checked" a total of three times. Two of these robberies took place in the restroom! Coincidentally, all cases involved a friendly approach to borrow a dollar, a vigorous plea to give up my cash, a forceful explanation to make me feel pity— as though I have some kind of obligation to hand over money, and finally an explosion of threats that sent my mind into a state of chaos. Probably the most irritating aspect of being robbed in the restroom is the whole unsettling awkwardness of the situation. It's filthy and has the repulsive smell of sewage, one which says "Wait till you're at home; don't come in here." I'm surprised at the villains who would spend an entire fifty-five-minute class period in the urine-ridden room, just waiting for their next victim.

The scheme usually starts out with a casual line, like, "Hey, how you doing? You got a dollar I can borrow?"—as though we're friends, despite the fact that we've just met and they're aiming for my wallet. Some of them would even attempt to build up a one-minute bond, in order to lure me into giving them money out of friendship. If that fails, next comes the moping puppy-like attitude that aims to evoke pity. Finally, their last resorts are the outright threats that erase my confusion and slam me into a state of realization that a) I am about to get beaten up and have my pockets searched for the money I thought I had so well hidden; or b) I am about to obediently hand over everything I have, and lose my cash along with my dignity. In the end, the result is the same. I walk out of the graffiti-decorated room feeling like my humanity has been torn from me.

Had my five-foot-tall, 110-pound body created an irresistible urge in the eyes of the attackers to steal my money? Or was it because my body, attached to a Chinese culture wrapped in an enigma of identity, suggests that I am a feeble rich kid? In any case, hatred grew within me, not only because the attackers stole the $1.30 that I was going to spend on my lunch milk, but also because all three attackers judged me as just another victim.

Over time, I began to feel a sense of disdain boiling inside me. My eyes filled with hate each time I saw *them*—them being the attackers and those who looked like them. I avoided all of them in any way I could. I walked across the street when I saw them. I did not make eye contact. I began to shoot daggers into their souls. I did everything to lose them in the blur of the world.

But simple evasive tactics were not enough. The reality still remained, *they* were in this world with me whether I liked it or not. Should I continue living a life of fear, constantly bringing two friends with me to the restroom each time I drank too much water? Or should I avoid the enemy altogether? I knew there was no obvious solution.

I now question what I felt after the incidents took place. I felt hate, a coiling strain of anger. But the reason for this feeling was still unclear. All of the attackers were of the same race. Was it an ethnic issue, perhaps? Would I have felt any differently if the assailants were the same race as myself? I rewound my thoughts and analyzed the source of my hatred.

I began to think back to all the times *they* were in my life, all the times I worked with *them* in class, played with *them* during recess, saw *them* every morning in my neighborhood. I thought I have been so easily deceived, distracted by their innocence, and duped into thinking that they were inculpable.

One day the teacher assigned partners in class. I was assigned to one of *them*. It did not come to me directly what he was. But as we worked together I began to realize that he was my age, in my grade, learning in my class. He was tall, skinny, and resembled the attackers, and yet he was not one of them. He was a student just like me, but a different race, once thought of as my enemy.

Afterward, I realized that my anger of being violated had overcome my sense of truth. I allowed a series of robberies to force me to generalize a race as being villainous. Gradually I began to change. I was no longer compelled to avoid them. The sight of them no longer struck fear into my heart, but was instead related to a memory of an incident from the past. I began to talk, interact, and socialize with them. I opened my mind into acceptance, with a new awareness that people simply cannot be judged with the eye alone.

JESSICA'S *NEWS AND TIMES*

by Jessica Ramirez

[*News and Times* Editor's note: This is my ideal newspaper. All the good news is displayed on the front page, and all the bad news is at the bottom in small print.] —J.R.

NEWS AND TIMES	Volume 1, Issue 1
San Francisco	Newsletter Date: May 2004

YELLOW DAISIES BLOOMING

—On a sunny afternoon there is a lot going on in the busy town of San Francisco! Here under the sunny bright morning on beautiful hills the smell of yellow daisies is growing in the Bernal Heights district. This is strange, because it's rumored that nothing grows up there. Some see nothing strange about this because they're caught up in what's going on with the war. I'm here to remind people that there's a lot more going on than war. Wake up, people, and smell the fresh air! Look around you: There are people falling in love everywhere. There are people enjoying life to the fullest, not paying attention to all the bad stuff all the time. There are people with each other, and loving each other day by day—like my grandparents! THERE IS STILL HOPE OUT THERE.

LOCAL GIRL IN LOVE

—In the meantime, here's a story about a young girl who fell in love with the wrong person two times. While the story might sound sad, it actually has a bright and happy ending. The story begins with a young girl who wishes to be happy, and strives to find "the one" at the early age of fourteen. Impossible for many but possible for her; she believed. Lucky her, she met the perfect guy. They became friends and fell in love. It wasn't normal for her to rush into a relationship, and she felt things were moving too fast. They broke up in less than two weeks. Crying in her best friend's arms, she lay there until she couldn't cry anymore. In the end, she realized how lucky she was to have friends and not need that guy! Now it's been four months, and both of them are happy knowing that they made the right choice.

Life is about choices: Don't try to run away from them.

UNDER THE WEATHER? HOPE FOR A CLEAR BLUE SKY

—The fog and rain are washing away everything. Over the hills, as the rain begins to stop, the sun starts to rise and a rainbow appears. As the rainbow appears, smiles then appear on the townspeople. Although it is known that you shouldn't look up at the rainbow because you can get a little ball in your eye that can eventually cause pain, the townspeople seem not to care, and they ignore the superstition. Happy people dance all around, everywhere, because the rainbow means good times.

TEENAGE BOY BRUTALLY MURDERED —BEATEN TO DEATH

—A teenage boy was brutally murdered by teenage gang members after being chased down near Mission and 24th Street. The boy was finally caught on 26th Street. The body was found by a woman who screamed for help. Terrified to know who the body belonged to, many were sobbing as they waited to find out. The body was later reported to be that of a sixteen-year-old, Jose Alvarez. The Latino community mourns the loss of a beloved friend, son, and classmate. R.I.P.

Death catches us by surprise, but that doesn't mean that's all that's going on in the world. Look around you.

TWO AMERICANS SHOT AND WOUNDED

—A confrontation between American and Iraqi soldiers has led to two men wounded. Thirty-year-old John Smith and thirty-five-year-old Thomas Jefferson were wounded, and now are currently in the infirmary—their families are being notified.

OUR WORLD TODAY

by Eric Yili Miao

The media today is filled with beneficial information as well as negative influences. People use the media (television, radio, newspaper, magazines, commercials, Internet, etc.) for many purposes. The media can be used to entertain; it can be used for personal understanding. It can also be used to get in touch with the world. In fact, the media was created even before television and radio existed, because the way a person expresses a personal idea or view is a form of media. The media subtly influences how we live and what we should aspire to. But for every yin, secretly hidden, there is a yang. The media can carry clandestine ideals that can have huge impacts on our everyday lives.

From watching our favorite soap operas, to dancing to our most loved rap songs, the media is everywhere. Americans today are so used to the way society runs, that even when we know something is out of place, we just assume that it's acceptable. The gruesome violence of movies like *Gladiator* or *The Ring* can affect the way a young child thinks. Explicit rap songs can make a teenager feel it is okay to shout four-letter curse words. The steamy and revealing nature of magazines can make young adults believe it is perfectly legitimate to have sex with whomever they choose. A person can resist destructive influences from the media once in a while, but if that person is continuously pressured with a certain view, every second of every day, that person can become hooked by the media.

There are over 250 million televisions in the United States, yet I barely see any good programs on TV anymore.[1] Positive programs that might reach us only capture our attention for a few seconds when we are channel surfing, because we're searching for that hot movie, or shows with danger, or nudity. This is because excitement catches our eyes and our hearts. Rarely do I know people who listen to classical music, even though classical music is known for increasing creativity and thinking skills. Instead, we listen to music where we just hear beats and inexplicable words. Lyrics are no longer as varied as they once were. Now, all we hear are the same words over and over again, and this repetition can pressure people to change their points of view. A lot of my close friends are willing to give up their cultures and styles just to fit in with the crowd. Pathetically, we are willing to change who we are so that other people can falsely like us more. Since the media says it's tight we assume that it's tight.

The media can really misinform us about life. In American society women are accepted only if they weigh less than 120 pounds and have bodies that kill. Women are brainwashed to spend thousands of dollars to look good and feel good. Men are respected when they have four or five half-dressed females next to them. Men are being picked off like flower petals and turned into wannabe pimps and gangsters. We are being told that we need to be rich to be comfortable, and with money, we are able to obtain anything we want, including true love. Media misconception even reaches youths who feel the need to date and have sex to be cool. The negativity in our media is what attracts us now, because good news doesn't even strike us anymore. But is there hope?

Peace and violence have always come hand in hand: Some people think that through violence, we can achieve peace. But Mahatma Gandhi once said, "An eye for an eye leaves the world blind." We cannot force a view on people and expect them to follow it. In recent wars, United States politicians have said we must fight on, we must fight to attain peace. Are we then trying to obtain peace through pain and suffering?

Then again, just because a nation has no wars or quarrels within, does that mean there is peace? Do leaders signing treaties of peace bring peace to a nation? Not necessarily. Because peace comes from within as well. Peace, then, is not only the absence of violence, but presence of God—the presence of unity and togetherness. That is how peace in the world can exist.

The media continues to pull us in a certain direction every day. You almost never hear about the good news. Each day's paper is filled with sadness and lament. Somehow, we manage to change the joy of good news into clouds that shed tears. Instead, we must try to see the positive parts of the news. There will be problems in the world, but we must approach them with sensitivity and a positive view. Once we begin to care more about what we see and hear, we can encourage more good news.

If we are careful, and become more aware of what we are absorbing, we can actually change the media for the better. Denying ourselves shows that don't really benefit us, even if we enjoy them immensely, is a good start. Exercising, instead of reading magazines about miracle diets, can also begin changing our views. More parenral oversight over their children's TV-watching habits out there will also definitely have an impact on our youth. A presentation of awards and celebrations, in honor of people sparking change in the media, would help jumpstart and motivate people to take action. But there will always be a supply and demand. If the demand is for more violent and sexually graphic shows, that demand will definitely be supplied. If a more peaceful generation demands more civilized shows and music, while rejecting negative ones, we *will* spark change in the views of media. The process will not be immediate, or simple, and the fight will take many people, but we can create a better world for our future generations if we are willing to educate one another.

Okay, now it's your turn.

---

[1] www.census.gov/Press-Release/www/releases/archives/facts_for_features_special_editions /001702.html

THE TRAGEDY

by Yuan Ting Tracy Lin

Sitting in front of the TV and watching a movie, I take for granted the fact that I am able to entertain myself on a daily basis. Sitting in class and listening to lectures, I take for granted that it's my fundamental right to receive an education. Hanging out with my friends on weekends, I take for granted that I can take a break from my schoolwork. Relaxing at home, I take for granted that there's a secure place for me to live. However, the world is not as peaceful as my life might suggest, and not everyone can enjoy the same rights and privileges that I do. I know that wars, conflicts, and violence occupy many lives. When I open the newspaper, I read about the conflict between Israel and Palestine. It makes me realize that there's no way for teenagers living there to relax, learn, and feel safe the way I do, because they live in fear and anxiety every day.

The Palestine-Israel problem became an international issue at the end of World War I, with the collapse of the Ottoman Empire, when Palestine was placed under the administration of Great Britain.[1] In the 1920s and '30s, large numbers of Jews immigrated there, mainly from Eastern Europe.[2] Palestinians demanded inde-

pendence and resisted the Jewish immigration, which led to a rebellion, followed, after World War II, by massive terrorism and violence
from both sides. Although the United Nations proposed the parti-
tioning of Palestine into two independent states, by 1948 Israel had
occupied 78 percent of Palestine and an even larger part of
Jerusalem.[3] In 1967, Israel took over the remaining territory of
Palestine. Two decades later, massive uprisings against the Israelis
began. Israel's reprisals resulted in injuries and heavy loss of life in
both camps. Although peace conferences were held again and again,
neither side would yield, and each conference was interrupted by
attacks and bombings.

So far, there have been some positive developments, such as the
partial withdrawal of Israeli forces and the beginnings of a democracy
in Palestine. But massive suicide bombings and military attacks continue. On February 11, 2004, for example, Israelis sent troops and
tanks into a densely populated refugee camp in search of Palestinian
militants. The mission led to the deaths of fourteen Palestinians, and
forty more were wounded.[4] The Palestinian organization Hamas
urged all its members in Gaza and the West Bank to retaliate.[5]
Judging by the past, we can expect that there will be more suicide
bombings in Israel in the days to come. The Palestinians call for huge
operations of martyrdom in the West Bank, Gaza, and Israel. Without
modern technological weapons, the Palestinians use their bodies and
crude weaponry to attack the Israelis, while Israelis have advanced
technology (and U.S. aid) for weapons.[6]

Among the dead in Palestine were some youths who were more
or less the same age as me. One had survived a missile strike on his car
in early 2004. In April of 2002, an eighteen-year-old Palestinian girl
named Ayat Akhras blew herself up at the entrance to a Jerusalem
supermarket. Reportedly, "she was not overtly religious, not estranged
from her family, nor associated with any radical groups. She was
young, a good student, and engaged to be married."[7] Yet none of this
stopped her. She'd been trained by Al-Aqsa Martyrs Brigade to be a

suicide bomber. The victim of Akhras's suicide attack was a seventeen-year-old Israeli girl.

It is very sad that women are killing women, and teenagers are killing teenagers. This is not just a religious war but a political war, using women and teenagers as a political strategy. There was another young lady, a mother of two children, who committed a suicide bombing which took her life, and the lives of four Israelis. I understand the anger she must have felt toward the Israelis, but how could she disregard her two little kids? Maybe she thought that being a martyr showed pride in her religion—that she would go to the heaven with glory, that she would help her country defeat its enemy. But killing innocent bystanders is a horrible way to express her feelings. She had two kids who needed her to take care of them and raise them. Now she is gone, and her kids have lost the person who gave them love and support.

Mothers, students, and children choose to be suicide bombers in order to supposedly "fulfill their duties." Both sides—the Palestinians and the Israelis—fight by sacrificing themselves. Don't they know that such violence will never ease the tension at all, but simply worsens it? Every time there's a peace conference, attacks interrupt the whole process, leading to the negotiations failing again and again.

From the research I did, and information I found, the friends of those bombers do not feel sad or miss them. Instead, they are very proud of what the bombers have done, and wish they could do the same thing. Even the parents of the bombers do not feel sorrow, but are supportive, because they lack any hope for change using any other method. Do they miss their children? Have they ever thought about the fact that, many years later, nobody will remember them? If I had the chance to talk to these parents, I would tell them that change must be achieved in more peaceful ways. I would remind them how important their children's lives are, and encourage them to find more positive solutions.

Youth is the hope for a country, for a group of people, for our world. If I had the power, I would like to be a friend to young Palestinians and Israelis, so I could introduce them to each other and help them be friends again. We're all human, which means we share the same hopes, beliefs, passions, and traditions. Only our cultures are different. That is why we should not be against anyone, but be friendly to everyone. I believe where there's a will, there's a way. The bridge of friendship exists, and the door of solution between Palestine and Israel is open forever.

[1] www.merip.org/palestine-israel_primer/brit-mandate-pal-isr-prime.html

[2] news.bbc.co.uk/hi/english/static/in_depth/world/2001/israel_and_palestinians/timeline/

[3] www.ifamericansknew.org/history

[4] archives.tcm.ie/breakingnews/2004/02/11/story133776.asp

[5] www.agonist.org/archives/cat_israel_and_palestine.html

[6] www.ifamericansknew.org/index.html

[7] http://slate.msn.com/?id=2063954

BEING FED UP

by Brittany Moore

Have you ever been so tired of something that it makes you mad, irritated, and ready to just say "forget it"? That's how I feel about the place I live. My neighborhood is a place where lots of bad things go on, and too many lives are being taken.

I live in the Bayview/Hunters Point district of San Francisco, California, where I'm a student at Thurgood Marshall High School. I like my school, I just don't like certain things about the community in which it is located. There's just a little too much violence for me there. Yes, you have a right to protect yourself, but some of the people my age have taken it to another level. They are killing each other for stupid reasons, and it's making all young African-American males look bad, when in fact they're not. And no one person should be stereotyped because of what other people do.

In addition to the stereotypes that people have developed about the young men in my community, some people have formed negative ideas about my school because of the so-called "riot" we had. In October of last year, a fight broke out, and seventy cops came; kids got hit, and some were arrested. They closed the school for a week, and because of that day, people have developed a negative perspective about our school. The truth is that they hear only about the bad things, and not the good. The only people who know the truth are the students, faculty, and some of the parents. I'm a senior now and I feel that my school is a good school and that I've learned a lot.

Living in Bayview/Hunters Point has made me fed up with San Francisco. I'm tired of hearing about people getting hurt and killed. A few months ago a girl and her boyfriend were shot at, and they crashed into my grandmother's cars. (Not one car, but both of them!) That's not the type of stuff I want to live next to, or start my adult life around.

Even though I don't want to leave my grandmother, because it's going to be hard, I feel it's what I have to do to start my own life and be successful. San Francisco just isn't the place for me. Don't get me wrong—San Francisco isn't all bad, it's just not right for me. If all the shooting and killing in my neighborhood doesn't stop, there's going to be no one left.

NOT SO PLEASANT HERE

by Diana Uriarte

For thirteen years I lived in a neighborhood where every morning I would see the same people going to school, walking their dogs, or having coffee before going to work. There was a tree in front of every house, and no building was more than three stories high. Each house had a backyard that met with everybody else's backyard, making it look, from a bird's eye view, like a park. It may sound like the ideal suburban neighborhood, like the one from the movie *Pleasantville*, but the truth is that I lived in the Mission District of San Francisco. Unlike the stereotype of urban areas, it was, for the most part, calm, peaceful, and a place where I felt safe.

I lived on a hill, on the third floor of my building, where I could see the backyards of every one of my neighbors around me. During the time I lived there I would almost always find the same people—neighbors were constantly coming and going. We more or less knew the people that lived in our building, we said "hi" and "bye" to each other, and with a few we would exchange gifts during Christmas. It was nearly always calm, and the only big thing I remember happening was a time when people said that an image of the Virgin Mary or

Jesus appeared on the side of the church that was right across the street from my house. It lasted only for a short time because, since the shape between the branches of a tree caused the image, once the tree grew, it went away. I can't lie and say nothing bad ever happened in my area. When things happened, it would be talked about at school. It made me feel better that people would react when something bad would happen. There were several people who got killed around there, but I felt okay because I would hear about it on the news and that meant it was taken care of.

I don't exactly know how to tell where a neighborhood starts and where it ends. The way I see it, if I pass by certain places on a daily basis, I consider *that* my neighborhood. I lived in the city, so there were definitely some things that were going on, but it just seemed to be part of life and, for some reason, I did not feel like I was in danger when I walked alone on the streets at night. I felt safe; and it wasn't just because I had lived there for so long, but also because the people there just didn't bother me. On my block there were two houses at the bottom of the hill. One of them was a small house with no garage or front porch. It just had a front door, and then a hallway when you walked in. Right next to it was the bigger house, where everyone would "kick it" on the stairs. It was two stories, with the garage on the bottom. The stairs were on the outside, and that's where the women would sit around while the kids ran up and down the stairs, and in and out of the house. The guys would be standing by the garage all the time, and some of them would be inside the garage talking, smoking, and drinking. They had barbecues almost every day, unless it rained or was too windy. And every day they would work on the cars they stole. These guys had that "old gangster" look to them, which was why they weren't very liked by the older people in the neighborhood, who saw them as hoodlums—the kind of people they didn't want to see in their neighborhood. I liked them, though, because they were nice, and some were fun to talk to. Even though they did drink a lot, and sometimes their friends would come by and act dumb, they never did anything too stupid. Although it may seem ironic, to me, they represented a sense of security. When I was younger and I would come home from school, I would pass by and talk to some of them. I felt that people wouldn't bother me if they saw me with those guys, because a few times when strange men would follow me, they would go away when they saw me talk to them. Even though it was true that they did do some illegal things and were—whether you like it or not—criminals, they had a different way of being than lots of these people out in the streets. They kept to themselves, and wouldn't mess with anybody unless they had something personal going on. Though some older people in the neighborhood were scared to walk by because the guys might do something to them, they really had nothing to worry about because the last thing these guys cared about was trying to rob an old person.

A little over a year ago I moved out of the city, about forty-three miles east, to the suburbs. It was a huge difference from the big city I was used to living in. In the city, I was used to knowing the people I lived around, just by seeing their faces every day. But when I moved to the suburbs, it was weeks before I saw the face of at least one person from each house on my block. Over a year later, I'm still not sure what my neighbors look like, and some I haven't seen at all; I just know they live there because I see their cars leaving in the morning and coming home at night. I live on one cul-de-sac where you leave the same way you come in. That limits the amount of people that pass by my house.

If you were to sit in my house staring outside the window as the day goes by, you would probably only see the mailman and the newspaper truck (not including all the cats that run around like crazy and some lost dogs every now and then). The people that work leave their houses around 5–5:30 a.m. and are home by 7–8 p.m. The only time you see anyone is during the weekends, when people mow their lawns, rake their leaves, wash their cars, and the little kids play in the street. If the weather isn't good—like during the wintertime—you won't see anyone, no matter what day it is. Because of this, when people come to visit or are looking at a house they want to buy, they think it's a good neighborhood, safe and peaceful. Then people get a false sense of security and slack off on their personal safety; many people leave their cars, front or back doors, and windows unlocked, and their garage doors partially open on hot days. They think that just because it may look safe, nothing ever happens. But things do happen, and it may be as safe or unsafe as the city at times.

I have personally gone to my neighbor's houses to try to get to know them, but every reaction I have gotten has been the same. Everyone looks at me as if I'm going to hurt them, or try to steal something from them. Sometimes, when I have rung my neighbors' doorbell for some reason, they peek through the window and make me feel like a criminal. I don't know what can be done to improve my neighborhood, but maybe someone will read this and get the message that they don't have to be so worried about meeting their neighbors. People always have the idea that the suburbs are always a calm and safe place, but are they better? Not for me.

VIOLENCE BEGETS VIOLENCE

by Zikang Liu

Throughout history, people have used violence as the most common solution to their problems. But the truth is that violence is not a real solution to any problem. More often than not, violence begets violence. For example, today in Israel the Palestinians bombed an Israeli bus. Tomorrow Israelis will attack Palestinian territory, and the next day Palestinians will fight back. Like a snowball rolling down a hill, using violence only causes more violence, and the issue gets bigger. We can solve our conflicts only through peace, not violence.

President Bush thought that, in order to protect our country from terrorists, we had to overthrow Saddam Hussein's regime first. In the war with Iraq we defeated the regime, and captured Saddam Hussein, but did we solve any problem? The U.S. military's victory in Iraq did not, and cannot, uproot the larger issue of the Middle East's animosity toward the U.S. Like a person cutting grass, the blades may be short today, but the grass will grow back again. We can destroy one regime today, but no one can guarantee that it will not come back. The conflict in the Middle East is deeply rooted within the people. The difficulty is not Saddam Hussein, nor regimes; it is the misunderstanding between Arab people and Western nations. Have we ever considered why those who crashed the planes into the World Trade Center were called "heroes" in many Arab nations? Have we ever considered why the people in the Middle East hate us so much? Before we can find a resolution in the Middle East, we must first learn the reasons behind the terrorist attack on the World Trade Center.

Since World War I, the United Kingdom, France, and the United States have dominated the Gulf region and its oil resources. The United States has also supported a number of brutal dictators in the Middle East. The U.S. supports dictators in the Middle East who make it easier to access resources in the region. The people in the Middle East know all about this, but most people in the West do not. Because of this, there is animosity toward America and other Western countries that is inherited from one generation in the Middle East to the next.

The children in the Middle East are brought up and taught that the United States and other Western countries are invaders in their region, who take away their resources by force, and show no mercy to their brothers and sisters. In 1996, when Secretary of State Madeleine Albright was asked whether the deaths of 500,000 Iraqi children (resulting from U.S. sanctions against Iraq) was justified, she answered: "I think this is a very hard choice, but the price—we think the price is worth it." It is easy to see why people in the Middle East, growing up in such a climate, hate us so much.[1]

I believe that, in order to solve the problems in the Middle East, we must first halt our military involvement in the region. During the first Gulf War, we reportedly killed more than 30,000 Iraqi civilians.[2] As a result of sanctions against Iraq, 500,000 Iraqi children starved to death. In the 9-11 attack, thousands of Americans were killed. During the current war in Iraq, hundreds of Americans and thousands of Iraqis have lost their lives. Like the snowball effect, the problem is getting bigger and bigger as it rolls. Violence begets violence. The only way we can stop the snowball is to cease our involvement in the Middle East. We exercised the power to start the snowball, now we must flex the same power in order to stop it.

---

[1] www.cnn.com/2001/LAW/06/04/embassy.bombings.02/

[2] www.globalsecurity.org/org/news/2003/030503-iraq-wars01.htm

FACE2FACE

by Adrienne Formentos

There sits a pinay in a room of every culture,
she stands up and out from her 4' 11" depths,
she begins to shout "Filipino Pride."
unknown what brought that about,
she then sits down cuz no one can relate
is this to be our fate?
she gets these questions very often.
r u Pacific Islander or Asian?
questions from all people: Black, Latino
      and Caucasian
she slowly comes to a realization. Wut am I?
people accused of killin' Magellan, short, dog eaters
and no way of tellin' us apart

No, u can't see me but I will be seen.
no, not in the paper, magazines, or TV screen.
but in the eye of the beholder who looks down
      on me

but will one day see... me
Face2Face

Put into that same category,
that same short, loud, got-long-hair story.
she'll close her eyes to try and deny those
        stereotypes,
the heat of the sun triggers the brain
        to run
to think of all tha broken dreams.
the sun slowly browns her skin
and she reflects on the person within.
she thinks to herself, yes, I am a Filipina
then a tear falls down her cheek
cuz the cause of unity seems a broken
        dream.

Yes, we got pride, but what good is pride
        w/o that unity,
that built our history? sick 'n' tired of talkin'
        hypocritically.
what good is that unified history when it's my
        own family talkin' shit about me?
a friendly kiss from Tita on my cheek opposite
        of what she will speak
when I turn my back and she begins that Tagalog
        shit-talkin' smack.
another one of those gossip folk,
but shhhh... it was not I that spoke,
remember she goes to church and prays
        tha rosary daily,
gee golly whiz, this world sure can
        be shady

Yes, we say "Filipino Pride" but what
    good is pride
when it seems like we give out
    bandwagon rides
to those to temporarily seek an identity or
another place to be in this Frisco City
where the hell is tha authenticity?

I head to the mall wearing a label,
    "San Francisco pinays,"
yes wit an 's' as in more than one person.
another Filipina sees my shirt and
the word branded on the brown skin girls thru
    out tha world
but instead of friend 'n' cousins lovin', I get
    dirty looks
and she starts muggin', askin' "who she think
    she is?"
I don't know, who am I? ain't that a shame?
from our cultured rich islands we came
only to divide ourselves.

Suddenly life ain't so great when
my brothas and sistas only know how to hate.
then our dream is just shattered,
poisoned by an image of what we should be.
resulting in a Filipino college attendance
    percentage of only 50
then cut that down by half and our
    paths diverge
then merge till it turns to self-pity.
mah brothas in fo' the thrill of a souped-up
    ride,

and pinays are the highest percentage
    committing suicide,
suddenly I ask, where is the pride?

But don't get me wrong, I am proud, short,
    no long hair but loud
yes, I am brown, sprung from the rich island
    soil ground.
those islands are part of us all, when we ask
    "who r we?"
the islands are separate but the people don't
    have to be.
there r those who pretend to be,
and those that utilize that fragile unity.
yes, Kansas comes to mind where
    an all-Filipino platoon
were the "Flip, F-L-I-P"
flip stood for "fucking little island people"
yes, those that take tha shit but flip
    the script,
rewind and "close" the switch

the people who remain faithful, tasteful
cuz we got sweet mango, bananas, sugarcane in
    our veins.
got guerrilla fighter's soul, Lola's heart to console,
    Lolo's brain for control.
got brown hair, brown eyes that always underlie
    the person within,
that person with brown, alibata tattooed skin
we fought for too long for all this to disappear
and only reappear when we feel like being cultural
    and Filipino

we fought too hard just to fall apart cuz
    we can't be united.
stand together and be one, be seen, heard,
    smelled, tasted and felt,
cuz I will be seen and
u will see me Face2Face

YESTERDAY, TODAY
by Jing Chen

Most people are happy, but nervous, on the first day of school, but I feel scared. It is the first day of school for me in a new country—America. Mom accompanies me to two classes. I feel better knowing that somebody is with me. In my first class, there are people who speak the same language as me. Although the teacher is speaking English, there is a translator who explains things in Chinese. But as I step into the art class with no translator, I take a quick glance and then go to the farthest seat because I do not want the students to laugh at me when I say something wrong. Then the guy from the next table asks my name; I tell him that my name is Jing. After that, he never speaks to me again. The teacher brings me brushes and paint. I start to paint on the paper. No one talks to me, and I feel like a loner. Finally, lunchtime comes and I hurry to the cafeteria. I find the Chinese students in my first period class and have lunch with them. Seeing faces I know makes me happy, but that time does not last long. Another new class starts. Just like in the other classes, I sit and say nothing.

The first day of school is finally over. I see my dad standing outside of school. I walk toward him and say goodbye to my new friends. When he asks me about my day, tears just run down my cheeks. My dad seems to understand me, and does not ask again. We get on the bus. I am thinking that I will never go to school again. But in reality I know I must, and that hurts.

I go to school the next day. I see some familiar faces. In class, I start to take notes and try hard to understand what the teacher is talking about. When I get home, I ask my parents if I can stop going to school. Their mouths form circles of surprise.

"I do not know a thing there," I say.

"No one is born knowing everything. We all have to learn," my dad replies. "If the first step does not work, try harder the next day."

I feel mad, and run up to my room. I open the book the teacher gave me in class. God help me, what are these words? Suddenly, the words turn into evil smiles that laugh horribly at me. I stay up until midnight. I regret coming to America with my family. I do not like it here, because everything is brand-new. I do not want to be forced to learn English this way. I do not want to live in this environment. I do not like this *at all*. God knows how many more days I will have stay up to do my homework this late. God knows how much I miss my friends in China. However, life must go on.

When I think of my parents, I know they are getting older, and are starting to grow gray hair. They work in factories that they would never have set foot in back in our hometown in China. They stand eight hours a day, five days a week, just to pay the bills. If they can work hard to survive, I know I can stand the hardship and do better in school.

The year passes, and at my middle school graduation I walk across the stage feeling proud of myself.

"I did it," I think to myself. "I am taking the next big step in my life."

After graduation, I start to have the same scary feeling again. What if I do not understand anything? What if I do not do well in high school? What if …?

I write letters to my friends in China, telling them how I feel, and the things that happened to me in middle school. They support me in spirit, from the other side of the world.

We can't worry about new situations all our lives; that would be a waste of valuable time. I'm now a senior at Thurgood Marshall Academic High School. I think about what I have done to achieve the new me. I can speak the language, and I do well in school. As long as I put the effort into my work, I know I tried my best. During these four years, I met a lot of people who have taught me many new things; they are caring and sharing. The road I am walking along is sometimes rough and sometimes smooth. Things don't always happen the way you wish. Accept it as part of life, and you will find more peace and happiness.

HOME

by Aaron Nievera

From learning the difference between right and wrong to under-standing the concept of fairness and forgiveness, home serves as the foundation for our education. But as we develop into members of society, other factors begin to take roles in the way that we are formed. Influences such as the media, history, and peer pressure shape our personalities, attitudes, and beliefs. And although these influences can serve as positive sources of inspiration, they can also feed our negativity, showing us the troubles and violence that plague the world. Whether we receive these messages of violence from print or the TV, many have been indoctrinated to believe that in order to resolve conflict we must resort to violence—turning away from the values we learned at home. History can have a similar influence. We see the violence that was promoted in the past, and still haunts us today.

As long as we continue to follow this trend of turning away from values and principles we knew as children, we will continue to struggle to find solutions to resolve conflict, and accomplish peace. We, as a society, must be willing to return to the things that were first instilled within us. Although it may be difficult to block the negative influences that have become a great part of our lives, to achieve peace we must realize that we have to balance these influences with the values that we were first taught.

Beginning in the early stages of life, children are exposed to the media and, consequently, to the harsh reality that we live in. As time goes by, and we are further exposed to the views shown by the media, some of us are bombarded with so much negativity that it becomes intertwined with our lives. In some cases, negativity overcomes every aspect of life. Growing up in the Philippines for eight years and being exposed to the images portrayed by television there, I saw, from a young age, the troubles that ravaged my country. From corrupt leaders to crimes that plagued the streets, I was exposed to many things that other children my age could not even imagine. As time passed, I began to see the effects of such negativity on those around me. Friends I had grown close to accepted the images we saw as children, and turned away from principles and values that we learned at home. It was then that I realized the detrimental effect the media can have on people. Images that we see can replace the values that were instilled in us, and cause us to turn away from the things that we first learned.

From the conflicts in the Middle East to the animosity that developed between the U.S. and Iraq after the first Gulf War, we see how historical differences and conflicts continue to affect our way of life. And, just like the media, such historical differences can also cause us to turn away from the values that we have learned. Before I took U.S. History my junior year, I did not know much about the conflicts between the U.S. and the Philippines during the Philippines' attempt to gain independence. From that class, I learned about the unfair treatment my people suffered as they tried to gain independence. As I became more exposed to the injustices done in the Philippines, I reached a point where they took control over my attitudes and beliefs, and allowed me to develop a strong disdain for the U.S. By being so wound up in the troubles of the past, I failed to realize that I had temporarily forgotten the values that I learned from home. My resentment toward past actions prevented me from remembering the virtue of forgiveness, and the concept of learning from the past to change the present. Throughout my life, I have encountered obstacles and challenges that have tested the values that I have gained from home and family. They have even made me forget about these values. Regardless of the outcome, however, I have always found my way back to living by these virtues and principles. It is through *my home* that I continue to remember and realize that there are other ways to resolve conflict. And it is through the guidance of my parents that I try to live my life according to the virtues that I have learned. As long as we continue along a path of withdrawal, we shall continue to struggle to find solutions to conflicts without resorting to violence. Although it may be a difficult and overwhelming task, we must somehow find a way to return to the concept of home.

TO HATE OR NOT TO HATE?

by Cristobal Gutierrez

There is, and will forever be, hatred in this world. There is, and will forever be, disagreement in this world. Violence occurs in schools, neighborhoods, workplaces, and everywhere you can think of. To kids in schools, violence or fights is a common thing. When two kids fight, crowds of people always gather around them and watch until the teachers come and stop it. Kids find fighting more entertaining than dangerous, no matter the risk. Two kids fought in my school last year over a girl. One of them risked getting expelled from school to fight for his pride and his woman. And this wasn't the first fight he'd had. He could have accepted the fact that his girl was with someone else, and he could have graduated. Unfortunately, he fought and did not graduate. This is an example of a tradeoff. He fought for his pride and lost his diploma. What would you have done? Is there a solution that can solve both problems? There is no solution for both problems. It's either one or the other.

Many people choose violence to solve problems. Some people react negatively toward others' different beliefs, because they see different beliefs as a problem. A major issue in our world is that people react to differences with force and actions, instead of trying to see eye to eye. Personally, I feel there is a limit to what you can or cannot stop. People often seek revenge and are always willing to get even with other people to make themselves feel better. There is no feeling better until the problem is resolved, even if it means to hurt someone worse than he or she will hurt you.

It is either love or war in any relationship. This is not quite like wars we have come to know of, such as WWI and WWII, but wars consisting of hate and anger toward another. We, as individuals, pick our own battles. We choose whom we hate and whom we like. It is human instinct to have enemies, in terms of beliefs, or lifestyle, or simply attitude. For example, I'm a peaceful person, yet there are people I can simply look at and tell I won't like them. It may sound harsh but it's just human instinct. I hate poets, break-dancers, and vegetarians. Why do poets say foolish things? Why do break-dancers make stupid movements to music? Why do vegetarians feel eating meat is so bad?

I guess the real question is: Why don't I like these types of people? I don't believe what they believe, and find what they do is foolish, but I choose not to react badly toward them. I won't go up to a person and say I dislike them. It's rude, and would probably make me look like an idiot. What I am trying to get at is that there will always be hatred in this world.

Every day, hate crimes occur. People fight, people argue, and people die. It happens every day. At night, I can't step out the house without fear of something bad happening. I could be in the wrong place at the wrong time and fall victim to hate crime, or a jacking, or a murder. For example, my cousin, my friend Peter, and I were coming from the store the other day, and we fell victim to a jacking. It was strange because right before we got jacked, I decided to leave my wallet at home and take only a twenty. "I'm not getting jacked, guys," I laughed to Peter and my cousin. Yet we did, and I felt sort of stupid afterward. My cousin says if we had bought one item less or one item more, we probably would have missed being at the wrong place at the wrong time. Nowadays, it seems a lot of ordinary people fall victim to violence.

Sometimes hate or violence may be the better solution to one's problem. I feel people will always seek revenge. There will always be death, money problems, and couples cheating on each other. People make mistakes, and people react to them. Everyone has enemies; if not, he or she will in the future. And one can't stop someone from hating his or her enemies. If someone hated you before, you cannot change that. To make them eventually like you is possible. Some people may feel it's easier to hate than love, and these people probably do not give back to their communities. These are the people who get off on making other people around them feel badly. Egotistical and arrogant people show themselves to others in ways that make other people react negatively. I can remember as a kid, a girl stuck her tongue out at me, and I stuck my tongue back at her. It was a sign of disrespect toward each other. If she feels that way about me, I'll feel the same way about her.

To have total peace can be very powerful, but I find it impossible to feel that way toward a person. Even if there is peace between two people, it can easily be broken. Sometimes a single word could be said to break the peace. The only way true peace can be achieved in such a violent world is by not acting so cocky, arrogant, and envious. Being selfless also helps, and acting with honesty and kindness will help, too. It is not guaranteed that the other person will have mutual respect for you. Presenting yourself as an equal to a person helps. You would also probably have to be perfect, so let's face it, there cannot be total peace. You, reading this right now, may feel my comments are idiotic; that's how life is. We as people view things with different perspectives. We can't really control someone else's opinion.

We as people tend to hate other people. We may or may not have a good reason why we hate someone so much, but sometimes it just feels right. I want you to right now think of a person you hate. Ask yourself why you hate this person so much. Would it be easier to be friends with this person? If not, you may have the problem. Even if you can't befriend someone you just can't like, it's okay. I guess you could say it was meant to be, and it is fine. It is just a basic human instinct. We as people make mistakes, we have enemies, and we do love others. People who hate, it is just their way of doing things.

INDEPENDENCE
IN THE MIDDLE EAST:
FIGHTING FOR JUSTICE

by Christina Khalil

I am a Palestinian-American who was born and raised here in the United States. Both of my Palestinian parents came to the United States in the 1970s to seek a better life. I have only visited Palestine—which I call my homeland—once. Over the years situations in Palestine have become extreme.

It all started in the late 19th century when Zionists showed up in Palestine to reclaim their ancestral homeland. Zionism is the movement based on the return of the Jewish people to the land of Israel. Jews bought land and started to build a community in Palestine. During this process the Jews displaced many Palestinians, and, in retaliation, the Palestinians reacted with violence. Israelis then decided they wanted their own independent state, so they went to war with the Palestinians. The Palestinians were forced to defend them-selves—which led Israelis to occupy Palestine.

Today, the situation in the Middle East continues. Unlike the common media portrayal, I believe Arab opposition to Zionism isn't based on anti-Semitism; it's instead based mostly on injustices com-mitted against the Palestinian people for many years. Palestine and

Israel are two different nations fighting over land, resources, and religion. Both Israelis and Palestinians feel that Palestine belongs to them—it is their hereditary "holy land." Instead of coming closer to a resolution, though, things just seem to get worse and worse every year. Israel possesses overwhelming military power compared to the Palestinians. Over the past years, hundreds of thousands of Arabs have left their homeland because of this war. Since the beginning of the occupation, Israelis have taken land the Palestinians believe is theirs, in order to build Jewish settlements. This guarantees Israelis a larger state, leaving Palestinians with a smaller area of land on which to live. Since 2000, 600 homes have been demolished, and 291 acres of land confiscated.[1] Routinely, Israeli troops blow up Palestinian houses and buildings, and kill numerous civilians, many of whom are women and children. Using American F-16 helicopters[2] to destroy villages, Israeli solders openly shoot Palestinians, and roll tanks into the refugee camps to humiliate them. Children are shot dead, and women and girls are abused.[3] Palestinian and Israeli civilians are sometimes unable to leave their homes because it is not safe to be seen outside. Mothers and fathers see their children die right before their eyes. Young teenagers fight back with only stones to defend themselves while Israelis have sophisticated weapons, airplanes, and military supplies.

Every day, Palestinians are fighting for their rights, and most of all they try not to give up their land. They go through great struggles trying to get through each day without food (being unable to leave the house as often as they'd choose, for groceries), and without seeing, or talking to, many of their relatives to see whether they're okay. Women in the streets scream and cry for their lost loved ones, while men gather in protest, fighting for their rights. The Israeli army has destroyed homes, and shelters for the poor. There have been hundreds of Palestinian suicide bombers who have given their lives in order to kill others. The reason these bombers exist is that they believe blowing themselves up is the most powerful weapon they have. I am not defending this response, nor am I saying that it is right (I strongly disapprove of suicide bombings), but in order for them to defend themselves Palestinians use the tactic of killing themselves, while taking a few others with them. If Israelis and Palestinians come to a fair agreement, there will be no more suicide bombings, or killings of any kind, on either side.

I believe that it is unjust that many countries, like the United States, strongly support only the Israeli side, which perpetuates a deadly repression. Israel has one of the most powerful militaries in the world, and the U.S. government provides them with weapons, airplanes, and military and economic aid,[4] which Israel uses to take charge, and leave Arabs in Palestine with very little.

Some Israeli citizens are also opposed to the war. Over a thousand Israelis have refused military service because they disapprove of the occupation.[5] Although there is some opposition from the Israeli side toward their government's stance on the conflict between the countries Israel maintains its occupation of the Palestinian territories, using its military power as well as its system of expanding settlements, checkpoints, and enforcing closure. I believe the main reason the United States is involved in affairs in the Middle East is, and has always been, to maintain control of the oil in the region, because this is the source of energy that supplies the industrial economies of the world.

The U.S. gives Israel an estimated 3 billion dollars per year (1.2 billion dollars in economic aid and 1.8 billion dollars in military aid).[6] The United States gives Israel all of its economic aid directly, and in cash, with no accounting for how the funds are used. From 1949 through the year 2001, the grand total of United States aid to Israel was about 91 billion dollars. Although Israel is only .001 percent of the world's population,[7] it receives approximately one-third of the American foreign aid budget,[8] even though it already has one of the highest incomes in the world.[9] From 1949 until the beginning of 1997, United States gave Israel over 84 billion dollars in aid.[10] This means that the United States has given more federal aid to an Israeli citizen in a given year than it has given to an average American citizen.[11] While Israel gets everything they wish for from the U.S., the Palestinians are given absolutely nothing. It angers me that the U.S.— *my*—government is giving billions of dollars to a country that uses its money for strengthening its military, and the oppression of the Palestinian people.

Every day, Israeli forces in the West Bank and Gaza violate many articles of the 4th Geneva Convention on Human Rights,[12] an agreement that governs wartime rules. Palestinian homes and agriculture fields are routinely demolished to make way for illegal Israeli settlements. Palestinians are denied various welfare benefits, access to many jobs, and the freedom to live in their homes because the land is under the occupation of the Israelis. For security and religious reasons, Israel also controls all external and internal borders, crossing-points, and major roads.[15] The Israeli government has developed a system for issuing color-coded identification cards and automobile plates, which restrict travel for many Palestinians.[16] Palestinians in the West Bank are often prevented from traveling to the Gaza Strip because they have to travel through Israeli territory.[17] Israeli security harasses and abuses Palestinian pedestrians and drivers who attempt to pass through more than 130 Israeli checkpoints.[18] For the Palestinians who do have jobs, 90 percent must travel through Jewish towns for employment. The United States is fully aware of the Israeli army's human rights violations, and is allowing weapons to be used against civilian populations in violation of the United States' own laws. While most of the world strongly condemns Israel's occupation of Palestinian territory, our government provides political and diplomatic support for the occupation to continue.

In large part, I blame the media for hiding what really goes on in Palestine. We hear news that Israelis have been killed or that there are Palestinian suicide bombings, but when Arabs die, we hear next to nothing. I don't blame the American people here in the United States for not knowing; I blame media for hiding the real truth. The media paints an unflattering picture of Arabs, but actually Arabs are the ones suffering the most. I am an Arab-American, and I know that, here in the United States, Arabs are struggling, because we fear that other Americans are blaming us, and calling us "terrorists." It makes me really angry that the Arabs are out there in Palestine trying to get through each day—they're the ones getting hurt, while America and other countries do nothing about the situation. We need to do something about this: something to stop all this hatred.

Palestinians are being herded like animals, and they do not deserve this. We are all humans in this world, and humans are not to be treated like animals. The children in Palestine are not living children's lives; it's like they are being punished—and for what? I would like to see children in Palestine going to the park, running around, having fun just like ordinary kids; and most of all, I wish that the children in Palestine would be able to go back to school so they can be educated.

I am very proud of being Palestinian, but sometimes I am terrified of telling people that's what I am, because as soon as I mention the word, I see the looks on their faces—how their eyes automatically open, with great shock. I'm afraid that they'll tease me; or, without even thinking twice, most will believe I have connections with Osama bin Laden. Honestly, I'd never even heard of this man before 9-11. What people don't know is that being Palestinian is a great honor for my family and me. It's really hard being an Arab-American, because I have lots of family in Palestine, and it bothers me that I can't really do anything about the situation there. It's hard for me, thinking that a Palestinian—right this minute—could be watching children being shot, fathers protesting, mothers crying—watching a life being raped of dreams, and being oppressed and deprived of freedom. And people still have the nerve to call us terrorists because we say "*No more.*" Not all of us are terrorists; our love for Palestine is deep. I have faith, and hope that one day the Palestinian people will accomplish the state of freedom that they deserve.

What I don't understand is why the U.S. spends so much money helping a country that occupies Palestine—spending so much money on tanks, helicopters, F-16 war planes, machine guns and bullets, all of which are used against Palestinians on a daily basis. I don't understand how someone has the strength and will to look at another person in the eye and kill that person just because that person is a different race, and because he or she wants the land. If it were my choice, there would be two states: Palestine and Israel—and Jerusalem would be an international city. Although the latest developments make it crystal clear that there will be no peace in the Middle East anytime soon, I still have faith that, one day, there will be. I don't support people being killed because of their race or religion; I just support peace, justice, and equality.

[1] www.commondreams.org/headlines02/0205-03.htm

[2] www.michiganpeaceteam.org/occupationfacts.htm

[3] www.miftah.org/Display.cfm?DocId=79&CategoryId=4>

[4] www.nimn.org/usaid/facts.html

[5] english.aljazeera.net/NR/exeres/D3462794-7857-4382-9EE3-A60ED1FC55D4

[6] www.encyclopedia4u.com/a/al-aqsa-intifada-1.html

[7] www.themichiganjournal.com/news/2002/10/22/Perspectives/Divestment.From.Israel.Is
.Imperative-303424.shtml

[8] www.wrmea.com/html/us_aid_to_israel.htm

[9] www.jfed.org/israeldiverse.htm

[10] www.wrmea.com/html/us_aid_to_israel.htm

[11] www.ifamericansknew.org/index.html

[12] www.scoop.co.nz/mason/stories/WO0309/S00028.htm

[15] www.unhchr.ch/Huridocda/Huridoca.nsf/(Symbol)/E.CN.4.2003.NGO.198.En
?Opendocument

[16] www.us-israel.org/jsource/anti-semitism/ot_report01.html

[17] www.globalexchange.org/countries/palestine/294.html

[18] www.us-israel.org/jsource/anti-semitism/ot_report01.html

I LIKE VIOLENCE

by Wanda Sarah Seto

The truth is, I like violence. I am not ashamed to admit that I like it, but that does not mean that I am a violent person, nor do I participate in violence. I was taught to think that violence is bad, although I have been exposed to a tremendous amount of it. I have always been fond of watching those kill-me-kill-you television shows and of playing bloody gut-spilling video games. They just fascinate me. I have played really violent games like *Grand Theft Auto* and I enjoy running over civilians, shooting all over the place, and watching the blood splatter everywhere. And just like anyone else who watches thrillers, I think it's funny to see the characters' terrorized reactions and how they suffer. Whenever someone dies in a horror flick, the audience in the movie theater laughs. This seems cruel, but it is not unusual. We can't abandon our need for thrills. We actually enjoy having conflicts and violence, because it's what keeps us entertained.

If I lived in a place where there was absolutely no violence, I think I would go insane. I don't think I could stand being nice, perky, and having lots of positive thoughts 24/7. In fact, I don't even think that it is possible. I can't stand being surrounded by "Pollyannas," those kinds of people who are so polite and so optimistic that it's like some idiotic clown is controlling their minds. I'd say that that place would probably turn into some kind of childish sitcom show where you sing songs and do little dances! I am not implying that this is a bad thing for *everyone*; I just wonder if that is all we're going to be doing in a world of absolute peace. Life is full of drama every day. The tensions between each and every one of us stir up conflicts and as a result: drama! Oddly, this is what keeps life interesting.

Throughout history, violence has been our source of entertainment. In ancient Rome, two gladiators would battle to their deaths while thousands of spectators sat in the Coliseum. Thousands of years later, people still thought that watching people kill each other was entertaining. During the first battles of the Civil War in America, people were so excited about it that they brought their whole families, including children, to the top of hills above the battlefields, to watch armies of men slaughtering each other. Unfortunately, these little picnic outings didn't last very long because some stray gunshots ended up piercing skulls.

Today we have the World Wrestling Entertainment (WWE). Fortunately, these big muscular men and women don't kill each other; instead they batter each other to a (fake) bloody pulp in the ring. I used to watch WWE when I was younger, and I have always known that the drama and the fights were all rehearsed, but I still liked watching people maul each other. However, if they were actually killing each other, I don't think I would watch it at all, because it is sickening. In the fictional world, it's not as terrifying to see people kill each other as it is in the real world because it is not real; it is just pure entertainment.

Violence has always been our source of entertainment, but that doesn't mean that people should kill because they think it's fun. At some points in my life, I have felt the urge to batter someone and make them fear me. Just because I have sometimes felt that way doesn't make me aggressive and it does not mean that I would run wild around the city trying to hurt everyone. In my opinion, having these aggressive feelings is normal.

Even though violence is entertaining, our society needs to realize that it is not something that we would want in reality. Real violence is not like a video game where you can have a "Game Over" and start killing again. It is very real, and those families who watched the Civil War only needed a few gunshots to realize that.

DON'T SCREAM; IT'S ONLY TV

by Duciana Thomas

So here I am in the movie theater, just like last Friday, waiting for the new action flick full of unnecessary violence and blood to play across the screen and inside my mind. Today it's *Saving Private Ryan*, and I eagerly cover my eyes and lean into my boy's shoulder, forgetting that every moment of this bloodshed was an actual event. I'm only seeing it as my entertainment for two hours.

And I forget to take in how it must feel when your body is tight with terror. What it feels like when the only thing you can think of is whether or not you'll escape. Not even taking the time to think about how people feel when they are so close to death, it's breathing on their neck. To feel that this is the exact moment you are going to die and nothing you say or do will stop it from occurring, not hope and not even courage. Just the sealed contract with your name scrawled across it that fate has chosen this day, this moment, for your end.

I remember when the made-for-TV movie, *The Elizabeth Smart Story*, premiered the same night as the *Jessica Lynch Story*. What angered me most wasn't even that they *had* movies such as these for the distinct purpose of entertainment, but that the TV executives actually had the audacity to compare ratings, as if they were just normal shows, and not the tragic occurrences of human beings just like themselves. That moment right there—my mom telling me about the comparison of the movies—inspired me to write this essay.

And you have to think, Why are these people allowing their stories to be sparkled in glitter and dashed across the country like a Broadway show? Why do they want their traumatizing experience to be viewed? Some want it because of the money, let's be honest. But maybe some actually wanted people to know what they went through, wanted their stories to be heard. So it's a sad, sad shame when the only thing that gets seen of these stories is the blood, guts, and gore. That the only thing we see is the knives slashing through skin or the bullets burning through flesh. And when we walk out of the theatre, or turn off the TV, the only thing we experienced was violence as entertainment—the true story left untold.

But it's not like I'm immune to violence as entertainment, or that I don't watch violent movies every other Saturday for kicks and giggles. It isn't as if I don't run to the movies to catch the new horror flick opening with as much blood as a hospital floor. Sometimes I hate it and sometimes I love it. I hate it when it's so real and actually someone's story. I love it when it's pure fiction. But no matter what direction my heart goes, I don't know what exactly to do with it. If I knew the answers I wouldn't be here right now telling you the problem, or I wouldn't be at theaters spending nine bucks to see exactly what I'm trying to rid the world of. I'm not here to tell you the solution, or tell you that violence is *oh so bad* and that we must extinguish it thoroughly. I'm just saying the way America exploits it isn't okay, and that's what we need to work on. We need to stop taking pain for granted, and start actually realizing that all this violence isn't just a movie or TV show, it's real. Once we figure that out then maybe then we can figure out what to do. Until then all you have is my opinion. Real violence shouldn't be exploited as entertainment.

SURVIVAL OF THE FITTEST

by Zack Farmer

(*Names have been changed to protect those involved*)

Violence has always been a part of human history. There is violence that is driven by anger, such as an argument that escalates to a fight. There is also violence that is driven by hatred, such as the 9-11 terrorist attacks. But there is a certain type of violence where fear is the driving force, which happens when one is backed into a corner and forced to defend one's self. In the animal kingdom, animals are most dangerous when they are threatened. I believe it is the same with humans. Some might say we have evolved past savage actions, but instinct doesn't change through evolution. Survival of the fittest is the most dominating factor.

In the winter of 2002, I became involved in a situation that wasn't mine to begin with. You could say I stuck my nose where it didn't belong. My friends and I were playing football, and one of my friends, Derrick, came up to one of my other friends, Nick, and started saying, "I heard you been talkin' shit 'bout me!" He started pushing Nick, and all of Nick's friends jumped into the melée to help him. I didn't want anything bad to happen, so I pulled Derrick out of the pile. But by doing this I accidentally pulled him down. He picked himself up and he and his friend walked off quickly.

The next day, Derrick came after *me*. And for what? The only thing that I could think of was that he thought that I pulled him down on purpose. The other thing I could think of was that the events of the previous day had tarnished his reputation, and the only way to redeem himself was to attack me. A teacher saw what was happening and broke the two of us up before anything could get started. For the next few weeks, I felt that I always had to look over my shoulder and keep an eye out for the person who was set on redefining his reputation.

The fateful day came the Wednesday of finals week. I had just left school with four of my friends. Derrick and his friend were not far behind. As we started to pass a local park, Derrick caught me, swung me around, and told me to fight. I tried as desperately as I could to reason with him, but nothing was helping my situation. He then took a swing at me and the fight was on. All I knew was I had to defend myself at all costs. I had to *survive*.

I was unleashed like a wild animal. I shoved Derrick's back right into a nearby truck and I used all my strength to ram my shoulders into his stomach. I even picked him up and threw him to the ground. At that point, I unloaded lefts and rights to his head. I had to be pulled off of him by one of my friends. I had lost all control. I feared for what might happen to me and I did all in my power to make sure that I would survive that fight.

Fearing for my safety allowed me to revert to the most basic animal instinct: survival. I fought because I had no other choice. When you are backed into a corner, instinct tells you to attack. Can you really say that we are much different from animals? We do whatever we can to overcome our fear, even if it means using violence. Survival of the fittest—that's what drives us all.

IS PEACE REALLY POSSIBLE?

by Marc Ang

The philosopher Thomas Hobbes once said that life is "nasty, brutish, and short." He claimed that each individual only looks after himself, and would only help another if he had something to gain by doing it. Indeed, it is human nature to be violent, even if we're not completely aware of it. For example, a mother scolds and hits her child for being bad. While it may seem that she's only instilling discipline and the right values in the child, she achieves this through violent means. Ever since the first humans walked the earth, violence has been a part of their lives. It is, in a sense, one of the reasons they have survived this long. The early humans had to hunt animals for food and clothing, and even today we kill other living things for food and clothing, though we now use different methods than throwing spears and stones. Therefore, I believe that while we can learn to have more control over our violent impulses, human society as a whole will never achieve a sustained form of peace because violence is one of the keys to our survival as a species.

It is very difficult for me to believe peace can be achieved without any form of violence, because sometimes violence is what brings peace. War is a necessary evil. There has seldom been a time in history when war was completely averted. Although war may be delayed, it will often inevitably come. In many conflicts throughout history, fighting wars brought back peace and order. Woodrow Wilson, the President of the United States during World War I, called the American entry to the war a move "to make the world safe for democracy," and referred to the war as "the war to end all wars." Yet, we have learned that history has a tendency to repeat itself. Just twenty-one years after World War I ended, a second World War erupted that lasted six years, and claimed the lives of more people than the first World War. I believe that the only way peace was achieved was by the United States entering the war, and defeating the Axis powers. Before World War II, Britain and France appeased Hitler by giving him the Rhineland, and even Austria-Hungary, but that only served to fuel his desire to conquer the world. Only through fighting Germany and its allies was peace accomplished.

Though we can never have everlasting peace, I believe that some degree of peace can be achieved. However, the question is, to what degree is peace possible? History has shown us that even major wars only give the world a short time of peace. So what can people do to ensure that there is peace in their time? There are no easy answers to this question. I often marvel at how people give short, simple answers to the question of bringing peace, without realizing how unrealistic they're being. You can't just tell the government of a nation to make their military drop their weapons, or tell every person around the world to be nice to each other. If that were the case, we would already have peace. Rather, I think we have to use subtler methods to find a solution to this seemingly difficult problem.

In every moment of our lives, we have to make compromises. We have to choose one thing over another because we can't have both. I believe that making compromises is one way to bring some measure of peace. Compromise has always played a key role in politics, both at home and abroad. In most cases, this has been the only way people have come to a decision, because everyone benefits in some way. An example where compromise has played a key role in bringing peace is in World War II. The United States believed that Emperor Hirohito of Japan was a war criminal, and should be tried at a world tribunal. But the only way the Japanese troops could surrender was if the emperor ordered them to. So, in order to end the war, the U.S. agreed to let Hirohito stay if he ordered the last remnants of Japanese resistance to surrender. This agreement between the U.S. and Japan ended the war and ensured that no further bloodshed would happen. Compromising is not a very easy thing to do as people often have their minds set on wanting everything. But I believe that if people were to actually *try* (because that's the best we can do), they could find solutions to their problems, where both sides are happy, and there are no further conflicts.

Humans have violent natures, but we have something that every other living creature lacks: a choice. Unlike animals that act on instinct, we have the ability to think about what we are doing. We can control our violence instead of submitting to it. This doesn't necessarily mean that we can conquer our violent natures, because being angry at someone or something is part of being human. Rather, our ability to choose helps us accept the fact that while our violent instincts are part of who we are, we don't have to let these impulses control our lives. Our world can never be a completely peaceful place. It's not possible as long as human beings are around, because violence plays a pivotal role in our survival as a species. But at least, with choice, we can distinguish the difference between right and wrong, and make personal decisions about how we react to conflict. We can also teach others about possible ways to solve problems without resorting to violence. We may not achieve everlasting peace, but we can certainly do things to ensure that our world is a less cruel place to live.

MONKEY SEE, MONKEY DO

by Brandy Frazier

> *"Many men wish death upon me*
> *Blood in my eye dawg and I can't see*
> *I'm trying to be what I'm destined to be*
> *And niggas trying to take my life away*
> *I put a hole in a nigga for fucking with me*
> *My back on the wall, now you gonna see*
> *Better watch how you talk, when you talk about me*
> *Cause I'll come and take your life away"*
>
> —50 Cent, "Many Men,"
> from the album
> *Get Rich or Die Tryin'.*

Over the past half-century, everything from music, to music videos, to movies has had an impact on the way certain people live their lives. I've always wondered why. The answer comes to this, in its simplest terms: A number of people are easily influenced, thus they do what they see.

In music videos you see half-naked girls, wads of cash, cars, sex, drugs, and violence. These scenes contribute to young girls dressing provocatively, and doing all the things they see in videos. The same can be said for young men—they want the money, the cars, and the jewelry, which they perceive are all part of the "good life." To achieve this they sell crack, 'shrooms, coke, weed, ecstasy, and heroin. To lead this type of lifestyle, these young men carry guns, which give these young men a false sense of security. Movies and books are filled with these negative aspects of life. You see Arnold blowing up a building, and Tyrese shooting someone dead after cheating on his girlfriend, and smoking a blunt. These images, portrayed as entertainment, become blurred into reality for some.

The question is, what can we do? Music tells us about "killing that sucka" and "fuckin' that bitch." In movies and videos, life as a thug or drug dealer is portrayed as a lot of good with a small amount of bad, but in reality when it's that good it has just as much bad. Young people, in general, don't see the negativity in that. When they hear the lyrics, they think "that's cool" and they turn someone else's fantasy life into their own reality. Death rates are high, especially in African-American-dominated areas, because African-Americans are the characters that are being displayed as the killers, thugs, and drug dealers. Drug dealers vs. drug dealers, prostitutes vs. prostitutes… but the most disturbing one is child vs. child.

Do we ban these lyrics and movies in order to help our people? No. Why? Because they're entertaining, and they make money. Regardless of the impact they have on children, and even adults, they're still on TV, and still on the shelves. The result has been more negativity over the years. From dance-offs, to rap battles, to shootouts, these movies and lyrics have only become more explicit. Explicit equals ratings, ratings equal money, and money rules.

The connection between media and real life is that they can mimic each other. But the media exaggerates and glorifies the negative things we see, and the consequence is that people don't know the difference. They completely mirror the actions they see and they don't separate the sane from the outrageous. It's sane to want to be a rap-per, or just a star in general, but to be willing to kill, steal, corrupt, or sell your soul and morals is outrageous. No one's life should be that screwed up that they can totally demean their life for a shot at the glamorous life. The bad part about living this lifestyle is that it never changes. In order to change this life of killing each other and breaking the law, the person who is living the thug life has to want the change deep down inside. That person has to know what these people are doing is wrong and that they're not helping future generations with this violence and negative way of living.

People see the glamorous lifestyle, but they don't see the consequences. People should take notes from others' mistakes; they should learn that you have to work in life, but that the line of work you're in shouldn't require you to watch your back 24/7 and keep a gun on your waist.

> *"Turn your back on me, get clapped and lose your legs;*
> *I walk around, gun on my waist, chip on my shoulder;*
> *Till I bust a clip in your face, pussy, this beef ain't over."*
>
> —50 Cent

But it's never over. We continue to live in fear for our young men and women and it's mostly because of the egos of our young men and women. How do we change this?

I hope to open the eyes of many people who may read this. I want to help African-Americans become better, and to build self-established communities with better goals.

Right now the world is a battleground—whether it's race against race, or set against set ("set" meaning a group of people from one place). Movies, music videos, and music have all helped to mold our community into a negative reality. People in the entertainment industry like to say it's not their fault, that they are simply mirroring what they see. While that may be true to an extent, they, like us, know that they bring out the worst in an already bad situation and then try to candy coat it to make it appealing to our eyes. And we mimic what we see in the media. The difference is we end up with the death rates, the loss of family members, the negative reputation—and they get ratings and money.

The only true solution to our nationwide problem is that we, as a people, need to look deep within ourselves and ask, "Is this what we want?" We can't expect everyone to change overnight and to evolve into a greater community instantly. But we have to, I implore, begin to lay the foundation and take baby steps toward this evolution, or we will continue to spiral haplessly into the abyss.

Let's evaluate.

WHAT WE SEE!

by Gaylon Logan III

Listen up! Monday, October 12, 1986, 11:37 a.m.—I'm out of the womb. I wish the way it is on the outside was like the inside; I had a feeling so pure. There, my eyes were still wide shut, only seeing and noticing the blood running through my body, still developing in the mist of time. Once my eyes are wide open, I cry because my mom is so happy, yet she is in pain. I smile to imitate the smile I see on my father's face. Smiling, crying, moving, talking, yelling—these are the images that catch my consciousness. The outside I don't like.

Time flies as I'm getting older, and becoming familiar with society's ways. I take in the feelings, hatred, voices, numbers, faces; they will be assimilated inside my conscious brain. As a child, the images around me begin to establish a character, which is my personality. Everyone is programmed, just like the programs on your computer. You start to soak in knowledge; violence (if it occurred in your life), habits like getting up every day, going to school, and eating. The computer inside of our brains starts to create programs that store certain habits in their appropriate place. Peace is placed in your memory file—if you've had any form of peace in your life.

Society, though, displays images that are not fit for our brains, and sends big viruses that infect the "way we think and how we act" file. Our minds lack plenty of knowledge, so why doesn't the television display programs to enhance the way we think? TV, newspapers, magazines, movies, music videos, and song lyrics portray scenes of destruction that try to make you believe a particular vision of how life really is. The images that we receive create new thoughts that influence the mind, either with hate or love. Trying to see life as beautiful is challenging and frustrating because my consciousness has recorded images that are both deadly and painful. I find myself chasing the moments that relate the belief that this world can live with peace and not grief.

> This harsh life is not aiming to soak us with
>   knowledge and power
> It's simply showing us how to kill every
>   minute and hour.
> Teach our generation the mistakes our
>   ancestors made.
> Our community keeps falling, but some of us
>   want to live today.
> Our peace of mind, which we expose, is such
>   a blessing up high,
> But the images that we see constantly destroy
>   our insides.
> Nevertheless, it's up to us to change because
>   this life isn't fair,
> But that's the way we are raised, living with
>   hate and despair.
> I'm not complaining; I'm just saying, "Watch,
>   and beware what you see."
> The government and corporations are fake,
>   even weak.

Record an image of a scam portraying scenes
    of destruction.
That's an image of a plan to mold our mind,
    that's "CORRUPTION."
Yeah, I'm living, but I'm tired that some of us
    just don't get it.
So open your eyes, see the vision because most
    just ain't with it.
I'm not trying to blame my generation for
    acting the way we do,
But it's time to stand up and fight; don't let
    nobody beat you.
React just like that, but be smart with your
    approach,
The system is misjudging you, so you stand up
    and be the coach.
Too many problems in this world, but
    the Malcolm X's will soon come.
That's the day we will rejoice and unite
    together as one.

IF YOU ONLY KNEW

by Gregory West

Growing up in two different cities in my short 16-year life, I've seen, heard, and been through a lot—from my mom and dad separating, to having to adapt to a new city and new surroundings. The two cities I've lived in are San Francisco, California, and Detroit, Michigan. From my experiences in these two cities it seems like it's the same: different people but the same old violence.

In Detroit there is a large population of blacks. In certain areas in San Francisco, there are also large populations of blacks. But there also are Asians, Latinos, Samoans, and other minorities. I have very different feelings about these two places. In Detroit, it takes a while to get used to where you are and what's around you because of its size. It's not a bad place, but some people tend to be rude and discourteous just because you're from another place, or you're new in town. In San Francisco, its more of a "Hi, how are you doing today?" type of feeling. It's like you're wanted, or welcome, even though people don't know you yet. Something that is overlooked, though, is the violence that lies underneath those polite words.

Being young at the time I lived in Detroit, there was a lot I didn't know. Sure, I knew that people were dying and being murdered, but why? I asked my cousin about some of his feelings and views about the city he grew up in. He's also been a part of the "fast life" or the "game" at one time or another. One of the questions that I asked him was about the killings and murders that went on in the city, and why he thought they went on. In response to my question, he replied, "A lot of people are about their money, if you interfering or messing the flow up of that money then you gonna die."

Next I asked, "How do you feel about Detroit and the things that go on around you?"

"Either you're going to pick up a ball, go to school, or be on the grind, that's the only way a black man is gonna get his money," he said.

When I talked to him I heard, in his voice, the pride and sincerity that he felt for his city. He knew everything that went on there wasn't right, but he was also aware of what generally happens, and had insight about why. If he doesn't know anything else, he knows his city. Although I don't live in Detroit anymore, I still have some knowledge of what he's saying, and where he's coming from.

I know Detroit isn't all about drugs, violence, and money; these are just some of the things people think "The Motor City" is all about. The same thing goes on in San Francisco. The first thing people say when they hear about the city of San Francisco is, "That's where the Golden Gate Bridge is," and where all the tourists go. Violence and conflict are a big part of everyday life in San Francisco, too, whether it's someone getting shot because of where they live and the "set" that they claim, to someone being in the wrong place at the wrong time and getting hit by a bullet that was meant for somebody else.

No matter where you stay, where you live, where you go, violence is going to be around you because of the jealous mindset, and selfishness of some people. Personally, I think violence doesn't solve anything. My cousin, and anybody else who is on that road or has gone down it before, chose that life to live. If there really are three choices (like my cousin says—pick a ball, school, or the grind), then I'm taking the easiest one of them all: education. I say education because it's better than being on the streets. It's hard to survive on the streets because somebody always wants something from you. Whether it's your food, money, or clothes: Something! If you get an education—something in your head—nobody can take that away from you.

TEEN VIOLENCE

by Branden Fulwood

Teen violence has remained alarmingly high in recent years. This is due to many things, but is especially due to teens having a lack of self-respect, respect for authority, and even human life. Some teens feel that guns give them power. The news media, and local, state, and federal officials often blame popular music and television. But I feel communities and parents need to take a more active role in the lives of children to help control the problem of violence.

According to the World Health Organization's October 3, 2002 report, violence is among the leading causes of death for teens.[1] While nationally the crime rate is declining, from 1984 to 1994, 15–19-year-old gun-related deaths increased 222 percent.[2] It is shocking that, in one year, guns killed no children in Japan, 19 in Great Britain, 57 in Germany, 109 in France, 153 in Canada, and a whopping 5,285 in the United States. A 2001 Children's Defense Fund report shows that nine American children die every day from guns.[3] The Teen Gun 2002 survey indicates that more than 40 percent of American teens personally know someone who has been shot, and more than one-third know a teenager who has threatened to kill someone.[4]

My parents always tell me that when they were young they really didn't worry about kids carrying guns to school, because no one did. They did not worry about gangs, and had no fear about going into certain areas and being shot. A lot has changed over the last twenty years. While most teens today are law-abiding and conscientious, some have no respect for anything, and some teenagers have no fear. The singer Marilyn Manson was blamed for Columbine, but in my opinion, those teens made their own violent choices without Manson's help. Teens today need to realize that while a gun may provide short-term power, real power develops from making good decisions, and finding other ways than violence to resolve arguments and fights.

The truth is that carrying a gun does not make you safer. It actually increases the chances of being seriously hurt, or of an innocent person being affected. Carrying a gun can also make you do something in a moment of fear or anger that you will regret the rest of your life. Teens need to think about the grief they could cause themselves, their family, the victim, and the victim's family. Television or music can't make you pull out a gun and shoot someone. The media may give you the suggestion, but the act of shooting someone is ultimately your personal decision.

When teens hear rumors that a violent act or a crime is going to happen, they need to speak up. They need to find an adult they can trust and discuss their concerns with, such as a parent, teacher, counselor, or principal. If they fear retaliation, they should find a way to contact the police anonymously. There are too many young and innocent lives being lost today, and having the courage to speak up can prevent this. Teens don't speak up when they hear about violent acts or crimes that are being planned because they don't want to be labeled "snitches," but this should not be an issue when it comes to saving a person's life. Furthemore, there should be more laws in place so that guns are not accessible to kids. Parents need to take more active roles in the lives of their teenaged children. They need to know where their teens are, what their teens are doing, with whom they are doing it, and how they are going to do it. If there are guns in the home, they should be kept in a locked and secure place.

My parents are a major influence in my life; I know they are always there for me. They have taught me to respect and to love myself and others. They encourage open communication. I know that I can go to them with any question, problem, or concern that I may have, and they will listen to me. I have been taught the difference between right and wrong. I know that if I do something wrong there will be a consequence, so I have learned to make decisions based on whether I am willing to accept the consequences of my actions. Unfortunately, some teens do not have trusted people they can turn to when they have problems. I personally believe that if parents, school administrators, members of the clergy, and people with authority took the time to listen to teens and encourage them to make good decisions, the teen violence rate would drop and innocent lives would not be lost.

---

[1] www.who.int/mediacentre/releases/

[2] www.sacsconsulting.com

[3] www.ocagv.org

[4] www.ocagv.org

ANGEL FACES

by Yu Ting Li

I live in the most violent area of San Francisco—Bayview/Hunters Point. I go to a school where violence has broken out and was covered on the news. Two groups of students had a fight that caused police officers to surround the street. The school was closed for a few days. My teacher was in court. All the attention of San Francisco was focused on our school. In the eyes of the city, our school turned from good to bad.

I live during a time when one of the most violent events in modern American history happened. It killed thousands and thousands of people on September 11, 2001. I was born in the year 1987, in China, when people were fighting for democracy. I have seen violence always being treated as part of the world's solution to its problems.

I remember, when I write my own stories in school, that teachers taught us that we needed to have a main conflict to make a story interesting. This is the same for books and movies; without conflict they would be boring. However, violence and conflict influence children because they watch it every day and start to think violence is right. They think the use of violence is the best way to defeat "evil" people. For example, Superman, Batman, and Spider-Man use violence to fight the bad guys, and they become heroes.

In war, soldiers want their weapons covered in blood rather than having their own lives lost. They know if they do not kill, others will kill them. Our government, family, and students today don't use peace because they believe it won't work against violence. Violence has become the most used weapon in the world. Yet, sometimes people do not know that peace is the best way to stop violence.

I was an immigrant in 1997. I was ten years old when I came to this new world called the United States. Since then, I have lived in Bayview/Hunters Point, in San Francisco. My friends, parents, and grandparents say Bayview/Hunters Point is dangerous and to be feared; it's filled with gunshots and covered in shadows. They also warned not to step inside those shadows for a second. I have lived here for six years and it's my home. In those six years I have seen different faces of Bayview/Hunters Point: the violent face, the evil face, but also the peaceful and angelic face that is hidden inside.

I remember one evening in December 2001: I was walking home late on Thornton Street. The sun had hidden behind the mountain. The sky was turning darker and darker and clouds covered the moon. The street was quiet and empty. As I reached the end of Thornton Street near Third Street, I heard a group of teenagers talking to each other. I kept walking down the steep stairs along the side of the hill. The streetlight above my head was dim and I could hardly see the path ahead, so I walked slowly. From behind, I heard a group of teenagers whisper, "Hey, go ask her." The word "her" gave me the feeling they were calling me.

"Hey," I heard. I turned around and looked at the girl calling me. She was big and tall and her long hair was tied into a ponytail. Behind her were two teenage boys. I had a feeling something bad was about to happen, but I was not alarmed.

"What?" I asked.

"Do you have a dollar?"

"No," I hurriedly answered, surprised. Her hand was like a tiger claw that tried to reach into my pocket and search for money. I pushed her and hid from her sharp claw. Before I could do anything else, she grabbed my gray sweatshirt by the neck. Then she asked again, "Do you have a dollar?"

"What are you doing? Let me go!" I yelled, trying to get away from her. I became nervous, scared, and could feel my hand and voice shaking.

"Let me go!" I screamed. But she grabbed me tighter and would not let go. Suddenly, she punched my left eye. I could feel my glasses press against my face. Then I became more scared because of her weapon: violence. I used all my strength to get her hand off me, but she pushed me to the ground, and her hand was still grabbing me.

"What's going to happen to me?" I thought. My brain was frozen. My mind tried to put everything in order. How did I get into this situation? I could not hear a word that came out of her mouth. I tried to yell for help, but there was no streetlight, and no one could see what was happening. I resisted, fighting as hard as I could. If no one could save me, I would save myself by fighting back. I had no choice. I wanted to hurt her and make her afraid of me. Then, I accidentally grabbed her breast. She let me go and walked away. A second later, I stood up on my feet, thinking I was safe. I had escaped from the tiger. I felt relieved. I took off my glasses. However, the boy behind the girl came up and pulled my backpack. Again, I fell to the ground. I felt the rocky street and my glasses under my palms.

There was no time for me to cry, or do anything. All of a sudden I heard a lady's voice calling from across the street. After that, the teenagers ran off immediately. I stood up and saw that a woman with a little girl at her side had saved me. She walked toward me.

"Are you okay? I'm sorry. If I had seen it sooner, I would have yelled at them earlier. What did they want with you?" she asked kindly. She was tall, but I could not see her face clearly because my glasses were folded in half in my hand. But from her voice, I could tell she was warm and kind, like a mother. She gave me a feeling of safety.

"They asked me for money," I said. Inside my heart, deep sadness was rising. I was glad that she had saved me from hell and pulled me back, and that she hadn't left me to the darkness. She gave me hope that there is peace in this world. When violence was harming me, peace saved me. Those fifteen minutes showed me real violence in Bayview/Hunters Point, but at the same time, they showed me the peace hidden inside. This experience taught me that violence could be solved by peace because the lady saved me without using violence. Instead, she used a single word: "Hey."

CHOICES

by Lily Qiu Ping Yu

"It's not my fault; I was born into violence!" How many times have teenagers used this line to get off the hook from major punishments for violent acts? Teens always have excuses for their misbehavior. Though it might be true that violence is innate to individuals, isn't it also true that each individual possesses the ability to control his or her actions?

Teenagers want to control everything that goes on in their lives, but when they get in trouble they argue that they can't control their own minds! It's an unacceptable excuse. They can't control everything that goes on in their lives, such as being in an earthquake or being trapped in a building. These things are out of their hands. But fights, drinking, or car accidents are preventable, with even a slight sense of responsibility and exercise in self-restraint. It is all a matter of choice.

Each one of us has a choice to be good or evil, to be someone people admire or someone people fear. Sure, you can say that you don't necessarily have a choice because of how you were raised—how you were taught to survive and deal with problems. But that is not always the case. For example, I have a friend whose parents are divorced, so she has to take care of a lot of household chores for her mom. Under more stress than teens my age might experience, my friend is still very kind to everyone, and maintains a friendly personality. Although some teens grow up in environments where their parents are irresponsible, teens still have the ability to keep themselves from developing violent behaviors.

The media, for example TV shows and commercials, often contains violent messages. Without proper guidance, teens may misinterpret these messages and be dangerously influenced by them. In the Korean movie *Volcano High*, students dressed in black and white—the usual cool image—fought against teachers to get control of the school. If parents don't talk to their teens about the main problem in the movie, teens will misunderstand the concepts of right and wrong, and, in this case, might think that disrespecting teachers is typical student behavior. If these ideas are allowed to manifest, they may lead to the imitation of violent and unpleasant behaviors.

You can make a mistake once, and argue that you didn't know what else to do. If you continuously make the same violent mistakes over and over again, there is no excuse. Teens learn from their mistakes, and if they really want to change themselves, they have the ability to do so. There are specially trained adults, such as counselors and social workers, who are willing to listen to teens with problems and help them find ways to control their behavior. If a teenager has even a slight desire to change, he or she can, with or without help. On the contrary, if a teenager doesn't have the desire to change, he or she will not change regardless of the amount of help available.

In order for teenagers to change their violent behaviors, they have to realize that there are other ways to solve their problems. Once they are conscious of the idea of nonviolence and try to control their actions, they can learn to be in peaceful moods when having to face difficulties, such as dealing with teachers or getting along with fellow students. But adults and parents need to convince their teens that nonviolence is better, in terms of solving problems, than using violence. Also, adults need to remind teens that not everything they see or hear in the media is true (though often teens don't listen, and most are likely do the same things over and over again until one day they finally realize their mistakes). When teens want to change, they must have somewhere, or someone, to turn to, or else they will just continue doing what they have always done. Adults should always have forgiving hearts toward kids, and help them make the right choices.

THE IDEAS
OF PEACE AND CONFLICT

by Brandon Williams

When we compare peace and conflict we see these ideas as contrary and far apart, but I believe that the level of conflict one experiences has a lot to do with the level of peace one seeks. For instance, if there is a fistfight at school, the peace one may seek is the fight being over. But someone who lived in Iraq through the war would seek an entirely different level of peace, like wanting the whole war to be over. The truth is that people only find peace of *mind* in the midst of conflict, instead of seeking *true* peace.

So when a security guard breaks up a fight at school, his only interest is stopping the violence, not in finding the root of the conflict. The reason people only seek temporary peace, or peace of *mind*, is apathy. And because of apathy they don't actually look for the solution that takes time, trial, and real effort. This is why I feel we will never achieve total peace. For example, a student at a school who feels out of control, or a young woman who feels that her neighborhood is unsafe, or even a person living in the midst of a war, may feel that there is nothing he or she or she can do, so he or she tries to find peace of mind and contentment, instead of an actual solution. This method of dealing with conflict is apathetic, and most people don't even know it.

Looking around, there is so much in society that tries to justify negativity. Whether it's on television, or outside in our streets, we all have witnessed the wrath of those offended. As young people, we hold the future in us. Unfortunately, society is not setting a good example. I believe a boy can't be a man until he sees a man in front of him. We will never run society the right way until we have an example of how it's supposed to be done. So, as I move out of high school and into adulthood, I will continue to look for what feels like the right way to do my part in the world, and be one fewer apathetic person in the world. That's one more step toward change for the better.

ACTIONS SPEAK LOUDER THAN WORDS

by Rosanna Lin

Our history is very important to our nation and to the world. It defines the past for us, so that we can learn and grow from it. The question is: Are we learning and growing from it? The answer may be surprising to some.

In a happy make-believe world, we say that our history is something to be proud of. Yet the truth is, our history has been based on a series of wars and violence. For example, there would be no America without the American Revolutionary War. That war was fought for independence, justice, and liberty. Yet after winning this war, the colonists continued to expand and that expansion resulted in the genocide of Native Americans. How could something that began with moral justification turn into something so horrible?

Our teachers, parents, and leaders tell us almost every day that violence is wrong, and should be only a last resort. Still, we have not learned from our history. The events of the past are still repeating themselves. We act as if it were our right to fight back against the people who have hurt us, instead of negotiating peacefully. We continue to fight other nations as a first resort and not a last.

On September 11, 2001, for example, hijackers crashed two planes into the twin towers of the World Trade Center in New York. A third plane crashed into the Pentagon, and a fourth plane crashed in a wooded area of Pennsylvania. Tragedy struck the United States and thousands of lives were lost. But what was supposed to be a time of mourning and sorrow, also became a time of revenge and violence. Less than a month after the attacks of September 11, America declared "war on terrorism." It seemed that the only solution was widespread retaliation for the wrong done to us. President Bush stated that U.S. troops would hunt down terrorists in a long, unrelenting war; not only for revenge, but to end "barbaric behavior."

On September 11, I felt sad, and powerless to stop what had occurred. I wanted retaliation and revenge as much as the next person. Yet, as the war on terrorism continued, I felt no sense of achievement or happiness. None of this helped me feel better about myself. All I saw before me was more bloodshed, terror, and deaths, and I felt horror at how we could have caused this much destruction.

This is the violence we experience every day. If we preach one thing, while our actions say another, there is not much to say about our country, our world, or ourselves.

YOU ARE THE PROBLEM; YOU ARE THE SOLUTION

by David Ouyang

Humankind's unique traits are its abilities to learn, create, and think. We use these traits to enhance ourselves. Human knowledge leads to power (such as the atomic bomb), but it also causes humans to be arrogant. When people are well-educated, they have the tendency to demean others who lack knowledge. Education has the power to make some people gain status and wealth while keeping others poor. The rich despise the poor, and the poor are jealous of the rich; it creates one of the never-ending cycles of tension. Once this tension reaches its highest level, it can cause major damage, even war.

Many people agree that violence is a dreadful problem, yet they cannot reduce or eliminate it. Violence is considered a sin, but I think for some, it is also a habit, a joy, even a hobby. Domestic abusers, molesters, murderers—there are some who enjoyed the crimes they have committed and they have the lust to repeat them. This incorrigibility suggests that these crimes are committed not because of social problems or pressures, but because the criminals may take pleasure in their so-called habits. I believe the simplest solution to reduce violence is to control these "sinners." They are causing chaos in the world, and I sense that one of their motives is to gain superiority over others, an example of arrogance. Violence is usually a choice.

Violence is separated into two fields: the desire and need. An example of the desire to use violence to be in a better position in this world would be teenagers fighting other teenagers to improve their reputations. An example of the need to use violence to survive in this world would be a man fighting for money to feed his family. There are times when violence is needed to survive. For example, when a police officer shoots an armed criminal. Or when a serial killer is about to kill again, then violence is needed to stop the killer. If the killer is not stopped, then the lives of innocent people will be lost.

Those who believe in a better world—without violence—are also arrogant, and it blinds them from seeing what violence is, and why it exists. People are blinded by their righteous indignation toward violence, and don't see that, at times, violence is sometimes necessary. The need to use violence to survive resides with mankind; it is one of the reasons why humans, as a race, are alive today. In basic terms, mankind practices violence to survive, and/or to reach a better status.

A possible means to peace can be found if war is created. Peace would not exist if there were never a war, because people sometimes don't understand what is actually a war and what is actually peace. One possible way to obtain peace is to have a war to resolve the conflict. It is a basic law of nature that, in order to create one thing, one must destroy another: One thing must die for the other's succession. Mammals gained power on Earth because the dinosaurs became extinct; if the dinosaurs had not become extinct, mammals would not have been able to dominate other species. Likewise, for a new peaceful society to exist, the previous society must be eliminated. For example, the United States has uprooted Saddam Hussein's old regime, and is trying to apply the United States' political system there. A peaceful society can exist in Iraq, but war with the old society is required. There is now no peace in Iraq, because historical issues still exist. Thus peace could be created only through destruction. Violence is part of destruction, but destruction can end violence.

To stop violence, you must put forth work and material, in equal amounts, to obtain a peaceful ideal. I believe protesters are misled in their thinking, and protest because they have nothing better to do. Their arrogance blinds them from seeing that simple protest does not have an immediate effect of ending wars. Just protesting isn't enough to end a war. Protesting has the same value as offering opinions to others, and the outcome will only be return opinions from the public. It will not get instant results. If a war is a possible way of obtaining peace, then protesting that war may not achieve peace. The key to stopping violence is sometimes to use it in a reasonable way.

Anyone can be critical with regard to any topic—the criticisms are his or her opinions. I have led a simple life, and have not encountered violence or war on a level that has affected me. I acknowledge the opinion that, not having experienced war or violence, I wouldn't understand the harshness of it. However, I have learned enough to understand that one of the simplest methods of eradicating problems is through destruction; and it may be the most commonly exercised in the world. We cannot stop or reduce violence, or war, without recognizing the sources of both. Violence and war will not end as long as humanity lives, because mankind uses violence and war to seek peace.

SALAAM, SHALOM, PEACE

by Yasmin Khalil

Violence, to me, is the leading cause of suffering. Violence is everywhere, while peace is virtually nowhere. If we were to list everything we know about violence, the list would go on and on, but the description of peace would be just a few words. Throughout many different regions of the world, violence and suffering have thrived for centuries. In Northern Ireland, for example, Protestants and Catholics have been fighting each other for years. In the Balkans, Orthodox Serbs, Catholic Croats, and Muslim Bosnians have endured a religious conflict that has left one million people displaced and 250,000 dead. But, in my opinion, the bloodiest battle of them all is the ongoing war in Palestine and Israel, where religious differences, and an extreme imbalance of political power, lead to daily violence and death.

Power is the key that opens the door to the definition of violence. All over the world, power is one of the reasons why there is more violence than peace around us today. The unequal distribution of power has people fighting each other to either gain more power, or to limit others from gaining it themselves. In history, we can see that, of all the wars that have gone on in the world, very few were fought for legitimate reasons. Instead, most were fought over who can gain more power than the other.

In the Middle East, we see an example of how power is unequal. Palestinians fight the Israelis on a daily basis, in order to get back the territory granted to Israel in 1948. However, with the overwhelming amount of power the Israelis have, this goal seems to be impossible. The United States helps Israel by backing them up with supplies and money, so that the power Israel has will wear down the Palestinians.

In this war about who is more powerful than the other, and which group of people is more dominant, little kids get stuck. These young ones are taught to go in violent directions because of their environment. In Palestine and Israel, hatred is embedded in the little ones who have not even reached puberty. These kids are put in situations, and taught to hate, for reasons that are unbelievable. Just like the adults, the distribution of power among the children of Palestinian and Israeli citizens is not nearly equal. Some of these kids stay up all night trying to make money doing all they can to support their family, while others live in luxury. When I visited Palestine a couple of years ago, I witnessed ten-year-old kids throwing rocks and stones at the Israeli soldiers who had set up checkpoints in the towns. I witnessed soldiers aiming and shooting at these young boys. I experienced what it feels like to have your great-aunt and her family have their home demolished because the boundary lines had changed and Palestine became smaller. And some say that the power of the two groups is equal? While one side of the country has all the land and riches and the other side nothing? Is that equality?

Violence is more than an obstacle, but it is something we all have in us. Greed, selfishness, jealousy, and hatred all come together to create the violence we live in today. To me, violence does not just mean physical pain, but also the mental anguish and disappointment that certain people have to go through. That is violence. Violence is when my mother is afraid to go outside to get groceries because she thinks she may be harmed after September 11. Since she wears a *hijab* (scarf), she fears for her safety because of all the crimes that were committed against Arabs, and especially Muslims. She worries openly about the welfare of my siblings and me. Before September 11, she always stressed the importance of having pride in one's self, and never backing down. After listening to my mother and her fears, I know that this tragedy got the best of her.

Peace is something most of us look forward to, but violence is more attractive to many people. If we were to be as motivated by peace as we are by violence, none of us today would have to suffer while we wonder what tomorrow will bring. My definition of peace is to never, ever feel like you want to end your life because the misery of violence has taken over you; to never feel unequal; to never wish you were someone different; and to never pray to harm someone. This is peace.

VIOLENCE—
WHAT IS THE TRUE CAUSE?

by Ashley Calloway

In my neighborhood, violence is something that occurs almost on a daily basis. I'm surrounded by a clutter of violence; sometimes, to get away from reality, I like to let my mind drift away. I like to think that I live in a quiet little desert oasis—a sanctuary from the trigger-happy chaos of barbarians. Because of what happens in my neighborhood, I've naturally become desensitized when I hear a gunshot, or when I find out that someone has been killed.

It was a Monday night, at around 11:30, and I was getting ready for bed, when gunshots broke out in front of my house. This time it shook me up, because it was right in front of my window. I heard glass break, and a bullet ricochet. I lay in my bed, stiff and scared, and my heart felt like it was going to burst through my chest. About ten minutes after the shots rang out, the police came. They conducted an investigation, and found that the bullet went through my next-door neighbor's window, which is just inches away from my bedroom. Luckily no one was hurt—just extremely frightened. Bullets don't always have a name on them, and my elderly neighbors could have been victims as well as I.

My grandmother always told me that as African-Americans, we have tougher skin because of the constant struggles we have to go through in order to survive. I agree with her because most of us live in the ghetto, and our children see things that no child should see: poverty, drugs, and many other things that are part of inner-city neighborhoods. Is this what causes some African-Americans to be so angry? Is this what causes our young people to be so quick to pick up guns and make somebody the next victim of black-on-black violence? Some say yes, and some say no. It hurts me to see my people struggle, and go through so many things that others will never experience.

The new trend that seems to be taking over inner-city communities is grandparents burying their grandchildren. It should be the other way around. People don't really understand what violence does to others. They don't realize that, when they pick up guns, someone's life is going to change forever. It's as if these people have no regard for life, and they would rather boost up their egos than back down and have someone call them "punks." Times have changed since my parents were kids. Back then, people wanted to resolve conflicts with a little fistfight. Now, people prefer to reach for guns. These situations almost never get better because there is always some sort of retaliation, and the same horrible violence just keeps repeating itself over and over again.

I've seen too many streetcorner memorials to those who have died, sidewalks covered with balloons, candles, empty alcohol bottles, and teddy bears. They go up before the memorials before them have been taken down. I've also seen too many people walking around with T-shirts that say "R.I.P. so-and-so," and "WE MISS YOU." When I see this, it saddens me because I wonder, When will all of this end? All I know is that, when I have a family one day, I don't want my children to be attracted to the so-called "glamour" of the street life, because there is nothing glamorous about suffering and dying before your time.

WHERE DOES IT ALL START?

by Suphain Htaung

I stepped into reality when I lost my childhood innocence. I used to think that life was peaceful, like a placid lake. In the beginning, I never had to worry about anything, because my family supported me. Most of the time I got all that I ever wanted. I received everything; I didn't have to think of where it came from, or how I got it. If I didn't get what I wanted, I cried. I cried until my interest moved on to wanting something else. But when I turned seven, I cried for a different reason: my grandmother's death. She lived her final days in a coma, and I last saw her pale face before her body turned into ashes. I didn't get a chance to know her at all, but I still cried, realizing that everyone will face death. It was then that reality began to glimmer in front of me.

I didn't live my childhood with an ideal family, where every member played his or her role in making a house feel like home. There always hung a foreshadowing of divorce in the family, due to conflicts. It pained me to face these struggles, but my family and I managed to survive the stormy days. Then I came to America. America differs from my home country, Myanmar, in that America emphasizes individualism. I was quickly exposed to profanity, and neighborhood violence. Though I wasn't yet ten years of age, I saw the realities of the outside world.

When I moved on to middle school, reality was again exposed to me. Fights every day in school were normal. Having police come to school when a gunshot was heard was another "normality" I had to accept. Normality meant being surrounded by people my age who were involved in activities that their parents wanted them to avoid. I knew kids who smoked weed and got high, girls who were raped or became pregnant, teenagers who got caught on the street for gang-related crimes, students who threatened teachers, and kids whose enemies were their own parents. They revolved around me, but I was not ashamed to call them my friends because, regardless of what they may appear to be, they always had something more than what was apparent on the surface.

I heard stories about dysfunctional families in which I saw resentment take root. This resentment started as a seed that grew *within them*, and their malicious attitudes scattered the resentment among others, like a virus. Those who had functional families, however, were envied, and felt ill at ease with friends of different backgrounds. Those who wanted to "fit in with the crowd" did anything for qualification, either by showing loyalty through the shedding of blood, or by transforming their identities. In either sense, they lost themselves.

In many cases, identity is shaped through the society and environment that revolves around individuals. Socially constructed power—in the forms of media, parents, friends, or school—impacts the identity of a person. Society encouraged me to dream, and the media displayed many role models who exemplified perfect lifestyles. For instance, I used to wonder about the enigmatic happiness that the family in *The Brady Bunch* always maintained. Were there always happy endings in family conflicts? Why was my family nothing like theirs? What made their family get along so well? I desired the happiness I saw in others.

Often, I wanted to wear the nice, expensive, stylish and carefully stitched shoes that guaranteed satisfaction. I fought for that kind of contentment, and forgot that my own pair of shoes had their own uniqueness, with their own vibrant colors. Like all shoes, they had their own purpose. Too often, I was caught up in wanting what others had. Too often, I was caught up in living up to parental expectations and not my own. Too often, I was caught up in living for the people I cherished and living a life for others. Too often, I was caught up in pushing myself to the infinite peak. Too often, I forgot to slow down and breathe.

In my high school years, I became conscious that I, myself, had a purpose in life: living a life for me. Reality had opened its doors to me and I entered questioning the paradox of life. Why do we do the things we do? Why are we living? After all that living, we'll all end up walking the same road to death, will we not? Life is given to us at birth and is taken away when we die. Life is simply a road, with a beginning and an end, that we travel in one direction. Truly, we've only got one life to live and to experience. But somewhere along the way of life, I got caught up in fighting to live, and forgot to appreciate all that I am. When I had moments to be with myself, moments where I walked and pondered boundlessly, thinking about my past, I began to appreciate my imperfect life.

No, I don't have an ideal family, or an ideal lifestyle. No, my childhood wasn't perfect, nor is the place where I reside. No, I didn't travel around the world, nor did I have the privilege to. No, I didn't get accepted to places where I sought education. No, I'm not the perfect student, and I'm not so innocent either. No, I can't meet all expectations. Nevertheless, I still appreciate my life because I've still got me, myself, and I. Even when I imagine myself in a dreadful place, living a miserable life, I know that my inner self is always there with me. All I need is to take a moment away from societal norms to get in touch with me, and to make a commitment to myself.

I discovered myself, and hope that you take a moment to know yourself, and view life positively. Appreciate the strand of life given to you. Any obstacle can be overcome when the mind is set with the right attitude. The right attitude is the one that speaks from the heart. Be true to yourself. We must learn how to be true to ourselves before we can find truth in others. Once that truth is found, it speaks a million wonderful words. We must find the peace within before we can increase peace in others. Everything we do starts with the individual within us. You have to love yourself, to find love's meaning, before you can *really* love others. In the end, you'll find that you never had any enemies to hate. Stop searching for peace in the reality that we live in, and *know* that peace starts within yourself.

THE REAL ME

by Eli Gualip

Violence can be defined in many different ways. It can be defined as a mental issue, or as a physical problem. Many people grow up with violence, yet don't know how to deal with it. Others experience violence, and learn and grow from it.

Violence is something I had to deal with, all my life, living in a house where all I saw was conflict. I had many issues growing up with violence, and I was really emotionally hurt inside. My father was "different," and hurt my family a lot. I thought it never happened to anyone else. I was taught by my father to be strong and never cry about anything. When I got hurt and started to cry, my dad yelled or hit me. He always told me that this discipline was for my own good.

Living at home was hell for me. I can't remember a day when I wasn't afraid to go home. I was always scared of my father because I was never sure what kind of mood he'd be in that day. My father had many different moods. When he got paid, he'd be happy and drink a lot. When he'd lose money, he'd also drink; and when he was like that, everyone had to get out of his way. Sometimes my dad would hit me, my mom, or my oldest sister, for no reason, and I'd have to go to school with bruises on my arms and legs. When someone asked about the bruises, I'd say, "I fell playing."

When I was little, my dad left us for a while and we ended up in a shelter. The shelter was located on Ocean View, and my first impression of it was not very good. I thought it was going to be nice and pretty like in commercials, but the brick building was very ugly from the outside. It was kind of scary for me. My mom took my hand when we went through that ugly door and I was not happy. But when that door opened, it seemed as though my whole life changed. The shelter was wonderful for me. There were other kids my age, and we didn't really know we were in a "shelter." All we knew was that we were kids, and we were having fun.

The living room was huge. There was a couch, with a kid jumping on it. The carpet of the living room was green, but not a nasty green. I also saw an enormous, big-screen television. I had never seen one that big before, and my eyes opened wide. It was at that moment that my opinion about the shelter changed. To me, this was a pretty place that looked like a hotel, and I was shocked that we were living in this place with such a T.V.

While living at the shelter, we first lived in a small room on the first floor. Though it was small, I felt safe, because we were together—just me, my mom, my oldest sister, and my little brother. I had so much fun living in the shelter. There was a little black boy, younger than me, whom I played with. My sister and brother played with any kid who wanted to play. I remember there was a small playground that had a slide, and one swing. Our room was next to the door that led to the outside playground, so my sister, brother, and I would sometimes sneak outside to play. We later moved out of that small room, and moved upstairs, which had bigger rooms. While we were living in the upstairs room, my mom got sick and had to go to the hospital—that's how serious it was. While my mom was in the hospital, we moved in with my mom's cousin. That was hell for all of us kids, because my mom's cousin really didn't want us, and her apartment was filthy. Also while my mom was in the hospital, my dad begged to get back together with my mom. He said he was a changed man, and that he would never drink, hit us, or leave us alone again.

After that promise that he made, my mom took him back, but he went back to being his old abusive self. I was growing up—seeing my mom getting hit by a china plate just because the food got a little cold, or watching my dad come home drunk and waking up the whole house. But I also remember watching my older sister find her voice. She began to talk back to my dad as if she weren't afraid anymore—but of course she was. So was I.

Elementary school was over, and middle school began. I was so frightened about the reality of meeting new people that I didn't talk at all. Well, I did, but only when they talked to me first. I kept to myself most of the time. Things got to the very worst point around seventh grade, when my dad went to jail for domestic violence. I had tried to kill myself once before that happened, and when my dad went to jail I tried to kill myself again. I was really scared. I was put in therapy for more than four years, but the therapy didn't work: I hated it. I would sit there for an hour or two, while the lady asked me questions about my life, nodding my head "yes" or "no." I didn't want to talk to someone who wasn't my friend, and who I didn't trust. She just asked me questions, and in the back of my head I asked myself, "Does this stupid ass even care about me?"

While still in seventh grade, I had this coffee-drinking teacher—damn, she was always smiling. It was so amazing to me: she drank a lot of coffee, but her teeth were still so white. This teacher was chunky—not fat, but not skinny. She wore sweaters that were made for Christmas, but she would wear them even in the spring. She had glasses that were pretty big, like the ones from the '80s, and she always had a smile on her face.

My teacher noticed that I was sad all the time, even when I thought I didn't look sad. She seemed to know how I felt. She asked me one day if I was having a good day. I just said, "It's cool," and that's all I said. Throughout that year, she asked me so many questions, and I answered them without even knowing that I was doing it. "SHE TRICKED ME!" That is what I thought, eventually. She was acting like my therapist, without my knowing it—I fell into her trap!

Once she kind of figured me out, she introduced me to poetry. When I found poetry, I wrote all the time, instead of trying to end my life. I could tell that my teacher really cared for me, and I noticed that poetry took over my life, because of her. After that, when I saw my parents fight, I didn't cry anymore. Instead, I started a journal, and I'd give it to my teacher to read the day after. My poetry ended up being *me*. I'd wake up in the middle of the night to write, and if I didn't have a pen, or paper, I wrote on the walls what I was feeling inside.

My teacher was the one who helped me with everything. Without her I wouldn't be here right now. No, I hadn't wanted to talk to a teacher about my problems, but I did it anyway, and it turned out that she was the one who helped me—mentally and physically. She did things that the therapists couldn't do. Even though I was in middle school, she made me feel like an adult. I will never forget that one teacher; her name is Ms. Reynolds.

Many would think I'm crazy, to have a close friend who was my teacher, but it is true. If Ms. Reynolds hadn't helped me, I think I'd be dead. I was one who survived violence. I would rather have people see me, and smile at me, every day, than have my friends—especially my family—visiting my tombstone. As each day passes, I never forget who helped me, and the *way* she helped me. I'm alive right now, and expressing myself more than ever.

I know that many people think they can never find an escape, but there are other options besides suicide. I've been there, and I know what it is to get hit, and to see my loved ones getting hurt.

When I was little, I wanted to do something about the abuse, but I couldn't. Now I know how to deal with it. I've been to hell and back, but I made it. Not getting hit anymore is like freedom to me. Not hearing the yelling, seeing the bruises, or feeling the pain—that is freedom. Freedom is great, and can be given to anyone. I really believe in God, and when I survived I felt it was a gift from God. I went through hell in my life, but I never regret it, because it made me a better person. I learned from all that violence—I learned that it wasn't my fault, and I learned how to make healthy choices. I also learned that the world is not perfect. I never ever let it get me down again.

I thank Ms. Reynolds for what she did. She was the only one who really understood what I was going through, and I'm thankful for that, too. I remember I was in her class one day, and she told me that I should sign my name and the date at the end of my writing. I said, "Huh?" And then she said, "You never know. Your stuff could be in a book someday."

March 1, 2004

ABOUT THE AUTHORS

MARC ANG was born in the Philippines and moved to the United States when he was eight. He's been living in San Francisco ever since, and plans to become an Army officer with a major in nursing.

ERICA BARAJAS keeps laughing and smiling, and always sees the beauty in everything. She never lets people get the best of her.

NIVIA BROWN is a 17-year-old San Franciscan who is not only living in the world, but fighting every day to change it.

ASHLEY CALLOWAY is a very loving and happy person. She is on her way to college this year and she will be studying to be a nurse.

JING CHEN came to the U.S. when she was 13 years old. During these five years in America, she has achieved many of her goals, such as getting into the college of her choice.

SHIRLEY CHEN is a nice, smart, giving, and caring klutz who loves her family and friends more than anything.

RICHARD L CHEUNG can differentiate very well between fiction and reality, but only in his dreams.

ZACK FARMER loves baseball and hanging out with friends. He is also a fan of the WWE.

ADRIENNE FORMENTOS is a Filipina-American poet with a voice, and is forever thankful for life's blessings.

BRANDY FRAZIER is fun-loving and loves to read and write. She takes honors courses, and dreams of being a famous writer one day.

BRANDEN FULWOOD was born in San Francisco, California. In his free time he likes to play basketball, and watch sports.

ELI GUALIP was born in Guatemala and came to the U.S. when she was two years old. She likes playing soccer, and she never lets things get her down. She loves the date 5/26/03.

CRISTOBAL GUTIERREZ was born in San Francisco and is looking forward to having a successful future, with no regrets in life.

MAURICE HIGHTOWER has learned to survive in a cruel world, but has not lost his SOUL trying to.

SUPHAIN HTAUNG is not just a rare name; it has many meanings, part of her name means "PEACE."

MICHAEL JORDAN is an African-American, Japanese, Spanish, German, and Navajo teenager with a unique perspective on the world—never bound to just one point of view.

COURTNEY KING is an open-minded, unique person. Wants to make a difference among teenagers through the health field. She's looking forward to her future.

CHRISTINA KHALIL is a Catholic Arab-American who has played volleyball and soccer for her school for the past four years, and is determined that one day she will become a sportscaster.

YASMIN KHALIL loves to learn about different cultures, loves the color green, and hopes for peace in Palestine, her home country.

YU TING LI is a best friend to Naruto. She wants to be as strong as Naruto, because he never gives up his life or dreams.

ROSANA LIN dedicates her piece to her friends, who have taught her so much.

YUAN TING TRACY LIN enjoys watching soccer games, likes to ask questions about interesting things, and plans to major in business.

ZIKANG LIU was born in China on June 11, 1986. He can't wait to graduate from high school, plans to major in Physics, and wants to be a researcher someday.

GAYLON LOGAN is an aspiring writer and poet who believes in the power of words.

ERIC YILI MIAO is simply humble.

BRITTANY MOORE is her own person, loves music, kids, and <u>hair</u>. She plans to go to cosmetology school in August of 2004.

THERESA NGUYEN is a Viet- namese-American growing up in the ghettos of San Francisco who looks beyond the limits and boundaries that are set before her, and reaches towards her dreams.

AARON NIEVERA uses music, sports, and life as his sources of inspiration to go about his day-to-day life. He, one

day, hopes to make a difference in others' lives just as others did in his.

TIAN JIN DAVID OUYANG, is a Chinese-born American (CBA), who has been living in the United States since late 1993. He acts upon the instant, instead of planning for the future.

JESSICA RAMIREZ likes to joke around and have fun, and hopes to become the nurse she always dreamed of becoming.

WANDA SARAH SETO says poems are her enemies, and plays the Chinese Yo-Yo with a group in San Francisco called Chung Ngai.

BEN SCHUTTISH enjoys play- ing basketball and baseball, and relaxing. He sends love out to all his friends, family, Mom, Dad, his little brother, Pete, and his girlfriend, Jamela.

DUCIANA THOMAS was in- spired to write this because of the low morals she feels the United States has. She says, "I think media is the main cause of increasing violence, and I felt that I had the right to express my distaste."

ALICIA TORRES is a dynamic

young woman born and raised in San Francisco with a passion for soccer and books.

DIANA URIARTE is a *Nicoya*

(Nicaraguan) who loves her family.

GREGORY WEST is a Detroit

native and plans to attend college after high school.

BRANDON WILLIAMS was

born in San Francisco and wants to become a humble example of a man of God.

ADREENA WINNFIELD, born

and raised in Hunters Point, San Francisco, loves God, her family, and friends. She hopes to be a chef someday.

LILY QIU PING YU would like

to get through high school without sweating, and through college without paying (as if!).